MURDER
—— *in* ——
MALLOW
A FATHER MURPHY MYSTERY

Roy F. Sullivan

authorHOUSE®

AuthorHouse™
1663 Liberty Drive
Bloomington, IN 47403
www.authorhouse.com
Phone: 1 (800) 839-8640

Published by AuthorHouse 07/05/2017

ISBN: 978-1-5246-9870-6 (sc)
ISBN: 978-1-5246-9871-3 (e)

Print information available on the last page.

CONTENTS

MAY THE ROAD RISE UP TO MEET YOU,

MAY THE WIND BE ALWAYS AT YOUR BACK,

MAY THE SUN SHINE ON YOUR FACE,

AND, UNTIL WE MEET AGAIN,

MAY GOD HOLD YOU IN THE PALM OF HIS HAND.

Old Irish Blessing

SPOT QUIZ ON IRISH SPEAK

(WORDS YOU'LL SEE LATER)

IRISH	AMERICAN
Acting the maggot	Acting foolishly
Arseways	Making a mess
Aye	Yes
Bogger	Rural person
Bumps	Drinks
Class	Good stuff
Cheque	Bank check
Deadly	Super
Feek	Gorgeous girl
Feeding biscuits to a bear	Easy
Feen	Male
Garda	Police
Gimp	Fool
Gobshite	Annoying person
Gom	Fool
Gombeen	Fool
Kerb	Street curb
Knackered	Tired
Muppet	Fool

Ossified	Drunk
Petrol	Gasoline
Ploughing	Plowing
Scald	Cup of tea
Shift	French kiss
Slash	Urinating
Solicitor	Lawyer
Spanner	Fool
Tool	Idiot

OTHER WORKS BY ROY F. (RF) SULLIVAN

"Scattered Graves: The Civil War Campaigns of Confederate Brigadier General and Cherokee Chief Stand Watie"

"The Civil War in Texas and the Southwest"

"The Texas Revolution: The Texas Navies"

"The Texas Revolution: Tejano Heroes"

"Escape from Phnom Penh: Americans in the Cambodian War"

"Escape from the Pentagon"

"Reflections on Command: Kit Carson at the First Battle of Adobe Walls"

"Killing Davy Crockett"

"A Jan Kokk Mystery: The Curacao Connection"

"A Jan Kokk Mystery: Murder Cruises the Antilles"

"A Jan Kokk Mystery: Gambol in Vegas"

"A Jan Kokk Mystery: Crises in Kerrville"

"A Jan Kokk Mystery: Who Killed Van Gogh?"

DEDICATED TO NANCY

ONE

In late October, cold winds from the Irish Sea sweep over the Old Head of Kinsale and into the province of Munster, warm and green since Michaelmas. Mallow, near the center of Cork County, still retained a semblance of summer despite its farmers preparing their livestock and meadows for the eventual cold snap.

"Hang me for murder!"

Loud expletives followed as the sturdy man slowly got to his feet after falling at the front gate.

His own front gate of *his* own white farmhouse. The door flew open and his wife hurried out to help him up.

"Are you hurt, John? Hush that cursing! What will the neighbors think?"

Dusting himself off, John Reilly chortled. "I'm fine, Kate. If the neighbors can hear me from two miles away, they must be Russian spies."

"It's not so funny, Mr. Reilly! Foul cursing and you on your way to church to a vestry meeting. Pray for forgiveness, John! Right now!"

Instead, the balding man stooped to retrieve his flat cap which had fallen on the grass.

"Damn wet grass." He replaced the cap at a jaunty angle, shut the gate behind him and waved farewell.

He didn't get far before her warning. "And come direct home after the meeting, John!"

This merited two replies: another wave from him and a slam of the door from her.

Still brushing off his knees and best tweed coat, he

1

strode briskly away toward the town of Mallow. The waters of the nearby Blackwater River gurgling over lemon-sized stones made a calming sound as he moved along, now noticing an aching knee from the fall.

"Wouldn't be wise to mention the knee to Kate," he cautioned himself, picking up the pace despite the pain.

Although he'd seen the town boundary sign hundreds of times, he paused to read it.

CEAD MILE FAILTE
Welcome to Mallow, County Cork. Population 11,600.

Turning from the river, he entered Ardnageehy Street. Soon the town itself was visible with the tall spire of Saint Timothy's standing sentinel behind it. He stopped to admire the view and check his watch. He was almost late to his first vestry meeting.

He hadn't wanted to place his name on the ballot, to run for the vacancy in the parish vestry, but Kate insisted. "They need a good, honest man like you, John. Boggers should be represented there, not just town folks.

She tickled his ear with a little finger, knowing his reaction. "I've already spoken to several of my friends …"

"You mean housewives?"

"Yes, John! And why not? They all gave me their pledges to vote for you."

"Keep the peace," he had muttered submissively, kicking at a large stone in the road.

Admiring a copse of alder trees, their branches heavy with red catkins, momentarily softened the thoughts of vestry duty.

"Ay, duty it will be," he groused to himself.

"Halloo!"

It came from the driver of an *Eireanne* bus pulled to the curb. "You're late, man, if you're heading toward that church meeting!"

Reilly stepped over to the driver's side of the bus. "Might you let me cadge a ride to the church, Donal?"

"Wish I could, John, but I'm twenty minutes late on me run to Fermoy." With a wave, the driver pulled out and headed away.

Although not as old as Mallow Castle on the other side of town, Saint Timothy's Church also looked like an ancient fortress. The gnarled roof supported gables on every angle. A jutting battlement protected the base of the church spire which rose some hundred feet over the countryside. Stout walls were covered with moss or lichen, barely interrupted by dozens of narrow mullioned windows deep-set more for thrift than appearance.

Maude Connor was the first to enter the parlor where the Saint Timothy's vestry would meet. She was always the first there, to assure she'd sit next to Father Murphy, the parish priest.

Her usual church-going ensemble was a severe black dress extending to the ankle, supposed to soften her short, pear-shaped figure. A small straw hat (worn every season), handbag and umbrella—all black—completed the uniform.

'It's my duty and due,' she often told herself. "I'm a Connor and my family's been in this county since the Normans. Besides, my saintly great grand father helped found this parish." Entering the parlor, she voiced it aloud,

3

just as she often did with newcomers who might doubt her provenance or high position.

Connor sniffed and made a wry face at the musty odor in the parlor. She marched straight to her favorite seat at the middle of the long table, sat down and arranged handbag, spiral notebook and pen. She removed and polished her glasses, then took a mirror from the handbag. Blue eyes examined freshly-permed grey curls which she touched approvingly with one hand.

The inner door opened so suddenly she was startled and hastily hid the mirror. It was the church sexton, wearing dungarees and gloves.

"Yes, Amos?" she recovered, arching eyebrows.

"Thought you should know that Father Murphy won't be here for the vestry meet." Amos grinned, seeing the small mirror disappear.

"His mother took ill and he was called away."

"Why wasn't I told before now?"

Amos shrugged and departed.

She exhaled. "Not the first time I'm ignored," she nodded, now checking pale lipstick in the reappeared mirror.

"Since I'm in charge, we'll get some things accomplished today!" she pledged.

The parlor door opened, admitting Mrs. Kennedy with her red shawl and cane. The older female used her cane like a blind person, tapping it across the wooden floor with every step. She was reputedly the oldest and wealthiest member of the parish, even exceeding Maude Connor.

"Just sit anywhere, dear," Connor warbled, hoping the older woman wouldn't choose the seat next to hers.

Mrs. Kennedy selected a seat farthest from Connor and sat down heavily with a sigh.

"Since the Father is absent today, I'm chairing the meeting, per his request," Connor said brightly, settling the matter.

"Haruump!" Kennedy grimaced. "Father's too smart to have said that! I've known him since he was but a boy. Always a bright lad!"

"Well, really!" Connor began crossly.

Viola Norton, the young parish administrator, hurried through the inner door. She began placing papers before each vacant chair. A green sweater and skirt accented her fair features topped by auburn hair worn in a bun. On the job for two years, she was widely admired as the most glamorous, eligible female of Saint Timothy's congregation, if not the whole town.

Mrs. Kennedy was quick to reinforce the question unheard by Viola. "Did the Father tell you that Maude would be in charge of our meeting today?"

Pursing her lips, Viola nodded, still passing out papers. Changing the subject she blinked at the two protagonists. "We must review this month's tithing report."

Not satisfied with a just a nod, Mrs. Kennedy cleared her throat. "Did you hear the Father tell Maude she was in charge of our meeting today?"

The parlor door was filled with a large, burly man, waving a hand in greeting. "Good morning all! Good morning!"

George Bailey brandished a misshapen hand injured in a threshing mishap years before. Despite the handicap, Bailey was the foremost cattle broker in the town.

He selected a chair beside Viola's and reached for his pipe and pouch.

Enmity unsatisfied, Connor turned on him. "No smoking in here, George Bailey. This church is a holy place, in which you should spend more time than in that bar down the street."

Bailey paused packing his pipe with shag. He looked about the room.

"Where's the 'no smoking' sign? Even the good Father lights up in here on occasion. So I will, too, your ladyship."

Someone snickered. The nickname was widely known but seldom repeated in Connor's presence.

Connor's scathing reply was cut short by the entrance of another vestry member. Businessman Patrick Davis, replete in suit, starched white shirt and tie, bounded into the room. Davis accumulated his considerable wealth in sugar beets before the European Union tariff.

Directly behind Davis, another figure hurried to the table. With a flourish, Davis held a chair for the vestry secretary, Joyce MacDoo, her hair just teased aloft like a fluttering dove by the local beauty spa.

"Here, Joyce, have a seat."

"Thank you, Patrick." MacDoo looked about, concerned that her hair may have been mussed by a breeze. "Have I missed a motion or a vote or anything?" she asked, opening a steno pad.

George Bailey raised a hand to Viola. "Miss Administrator, are there enough members present for us to call this an official meeting?"

Standing to count faces, Viola shook her head, frowning. "No, no quorum. Our new member, John Reilly, is absent."

Connor shook her head, slapping her notebook on the table for attention. "We'll wait for the absent member for five—no, ten—minutes before we start the meeting with the tithing report."

Patrick Davis stood, too. "Lacking a quorum, I move we adjourn until Father Murphy is present. I know him to be very concerned with the budget."

Mrs. Kennedy waved her cane in the air. "I second that motion. Viola, ask the Father on his return when can he meet with us?"

Viola stood again. "All in favor?"

The 'Ayes' were drowned out by the noise of the members heading out the parlor door.

All except one who remained seated.

Maude Connor.

She looked heavenward in exasperation. "Shanty Irish! They just ignored me as if I wasn't even here! They will regret this! There'll be a reckoning one of these days! And soon!"

In the hallway, Joyce MacDoo paused, hearing the threat. She put on her cape and left quietly.

Just as quietly a door down the hallway closed.

TWO

Outside Saint Timothy's, a sheepish John Reilly stood on the kerb as the vestry members hurried out the church.

"Sorry I'm a bit late," he apologized.

To his surprise, the group seemed forgiving, if not cheerful. Several patted his shoulder as they passed.

"You didn't miss a thing, John."

"Except a few fireworks," Pat Davis joked.

"C'mon with George and me. John. We'll fill you in on our short—almost sweet—meeting."

Across the street and down a block, facing Saint Timothy's like a delinquent communicant was their favorite bar. A big green and yellow sign atop the white-washed front proclaimed the long-gone proprietor's name, John Long.

The lone narrow-glassed front window was adorned with big, iron fleur-de-lis to keep thieves out and paying customers in. A worn but still-bright red double door was guarded by a large grey cat, usually sleeping in the sunshine.

Inside, the bar was dark, the air pungent with the yeasty odors of ale and stout.

"I'm buying the first round for my brother vestrymen here," Bailey palmed a large bill on the counter.

The barman paused while wiping the counter with a rag. "What'll it be, gents?"

Davis was first. "Guinness for me. Thanks, George!"

John Reilly happily asked for a Harp. Host George Bailey followed, requesting a Smithwick ale while accepting Reilly's thanks and handshake.

The trio tipped their big glasses and drank.

"So what did I miss?" Reilly asked, smacking his lips. "If them vestry meetings all end like this, I'll enjoy being a member. Best not tell the wife."

"You summarize the meeting, George," Patrick nudged Bailey. "You add the angry theatrics better than me."

"Well, we hadn't enough people for a quorum," George began. "And Father Murphy was absent, seein' to his sick mother."

"So Mister Patrick Davis here, smooth parliamentarian that he is, moved that the vestry be dismissed, to be recalled when the good Father could be present.

"All the vestry, being good souls, agreed except for Maude Connor. 'Her Ladyship' asserted her domination, made a face and said we must wait ten minutes more, then discuss the tithing report without the Father.

"All of us marched out of that parlor, leaving Maude sputtering in her chair."

George waved to the bartender for more pints. "I'll drink to that!"

And they did.

By early afternoon several more pints had been consumed and all the available bar food eaten by the once-thirsty trio.

Loosening his necktie, Davis patted his stomach, "We should make a habit of this after every meeting, brother vestrymen."

"Here! Here!" Bailey banged his pint against the counter. "A grand idea. And ask the ladies, too! What do you think of that, John?"

Unused to drinking in the afternoon, Reilly nodded, his

thoughts on what Kate would say when he returned home. Should he confess he'd missed the vestry meeting and that he'd gone—no, been forced to go—to John Long's?

"Let's retire to that table over there for some serious discussion," George Bailey pointed to a secluded corner.

John belched, holding up a finger to the barman. "Another round, if you please, Sean."

"Here's my contribution to serious discussion," began Davis as they sat down at the table. He related a story:

> Pat, all upset with his marriage, went to see his priest.
> *What's the trouble, son?*
> Father, it's my marriage. I'm so depressed. I'm leaving her.
> *Oh, no, Pat! You must not do that! Tell me what's wrong.*
> When I came home from a sales meeting in Cork, guess what I found?
> *Well, whatever it was, it's redeemable by prayer, son.*
> But Father, I found my wife in bed with the plumber!
> I'd even sent her an e-mail telling I was on my way home!
> Father picked up the telephone and called Pat's wife.
> After a short conversation, he replaced the phone with a big smile.
> *Didn't I tell you everything's possible with prayer, Pat?*

She didn't get the e-mail!

After the laughter, coughing and drink-spilling, Patrick Davis clapped his hands for attention. "Now I'm really serious," he began after the table had been dried with a bar towel.

"I'm for replacing that smug Maude Connor on the vestry by a young, attractive lady or gentleman who might enjoy an after-vestry drink with the three engaging gentlemen seated here."

"He means us!" George Bailey cavorted, pounding John on the back.

"Ha, ha! Getting rid of Maude would be as difficult as walkin' on water," George demurred.

"We'd accomplish more at those boring meetings without her, wouldn't we?" Patrick leaned both elbows on the table. "I tell you 'Her Ladyship' is a jinx!"

"But how can we ease her out of the vestry?" John countered.

Davis held up a finger. "Get Father Murphy involved somehow. Then she'd have to go."

As the drinks arrived, Bailey and Davis held hands on the table. "C'mon, John."

"Huh?"

"A solemn pact that we'll work on a plan to rid the vestry of Maude."

"Agreed," the three repeated solemnly, grasping hands.

The pact was sealed by another round of drinks and a loud chorus of a song beginning "There Was a Wild Colonial Boy…."

Assessing the condition of his mates, Patrick offered to drive them home in his Range Rover which he'd left behind the church. Happily they crammed into the vehicle and speeded through Mallow, horn tooting at every corner.

THREE

Stepping off the train at the Mallow Rail Station the next morning, Father Aloysius T. Murphy waved down a taxi. Soon he was standing outside Saint Timothy's and opening his wallet to pay.

"Nay, no need for that Father." The driver held up a hand as the fare was offered. "It was my pleasure. Welcome home!"

Murphy shook his hand. "I thank you kindly, Mickey. Hope to see you at Sunday mass."

"You will, Father, you will."

Mrs. Casey, his aging, graying housekeeper, met her forty-year old charge at the door. "Oh, Father! You're home! Welcome!"

"Thank you, Mrs. Casey. Good to be back."

The tall, thin man dressed in wrinkled black suit and clerical collar, smiled as he surveyed the old manse, his home for the past three years. It impressed him as solid and resolute as Casey, its housekeeper.

Murphy had been assigned to Mallow by his bishop after a harrowing tour in Afghanistan with an Irish Army infantry battalion.

As she reached for his leather valise, he stayed her hand. "None of that now. Mrs. Casey. You're spoiling me already."

She blushed. "So, how's your mother, Father?"

Murphy felt of his unshaven-since-yesterday chin before answering. "As fine as can be expected for a ninety-year old. Thank you for asking."

"Is she still in the Cork hospital, Father?"

"No. I'm thankful she's at home with my sister in Naas. When I left last night they both seemed to be thriving."

He glanced at the open front door. "What's been going on here?"

"Viola asked me to call her once you feel rested from the trip. Several people have asked to schedule time with you.

"Did you have your breakfast on the way here, Father?"

"I had tea on the train. But I wouldn't mind a cup of your good black coffee and a biscuit before seeing Viola. I'll take my things upstairs, shave and be with you in… fifteen minutes?"

Beaming, she curtsied. "Fine, Father."

As the parish administrator, Viola Norton had first claim on her priest's time, even ahead of parishioners. The two sat on either side of the small table in Murphy's downstairs office. After another welcome, she handed him a typed list.

"Organized, as always, Viola," he patted her hand. "I've said this before but it's worth repeating.

"Saint Timothy's couldn't perform its job—saving souls—nearly as well without you. I appreciate your thoughtful performance. I know our parishioners do, too."

The young lady beamed. "Thank you, Father."

"I see the first item is the last vestry meeting. Did it go well?"

"No, Father. It was a bit of a disaster without you. Everyone, beginning with Maude, wanted to be in charge. Our new member, John Reilly, was absent so we didn't have enough folks for a regular meeting.

"To frustrate Maude, I think, Patrick Davis moved that

we adjourn until your return. She objected and unkind words were spoken as everyone made for the door. I'd hoped to present the tithing report but didn't get the chance."

"Unkind words? I can't imagine our staid vestry in such disarray. What was said?"

Viola shook her head. "I hesitate to repeat it, Father."

"I'm sure to have heard much worse. Out with it."

She took a breath. "George Bailey called Mrs. Connor 'Your Ladyship."

Suppressing a grin, Murphy studied Viola's expression.

"And everyone, myself included, tittered. Please forgive me, Father."

"Well, at the next vestry meeting we'll begin with a short prayer about kindness and love for one another. We'll schedule the next vestry in two weeks, will that do?"

"Fine, Father."

Murphy moved his finger down the list. "Mary Canady wants to see me?"

"Yes, Father. She wants to tell you about threats she's been receiving."

"Did she inform the *Garda?*"

"Yes, Father, but the police don't seem to satisfy her. She called them anti-feminist loafers."

Murphy exhaled. "Then I'd better see her after her shift at the Coffee House today. Can you get word to her?

"Yes. Anything else?"

Murphy leaned forward. "I heard Mrs. Casey sobbing in her room several nights ago. Do you know what's wrong? She's usually so calm and collected."

Viola sighed, also leaning forward. "Father, it's her son. Seems like he's always in trouble. She told me he had recently been in prison. She's very worried about him. Please don't tell her I told you."

"Of course not," he patted her hand. "Do you think I can help in any way?"

Viola shook her head. "Can't think how at the moment, Father. Catechism class is still scheduled for Friday, if that's alright."

"It is. Usual time?"

"Yes. Next is a new item: Marie Sullivan and Ron Calhoun want to begin marriage counseling at your convenience."

"Not pregnant, is she?"

"She said no, Father."

"Fine, then there's no hurry. Put them on for next Tuesday evening after vespers."

'Father, I hate to add to your worries, you're being just back and all. But the roof over the nave is leaking again. I told Amos and he said he'd look at today."

Murphy had barely settled at his desk after touring the sacristy and parlor when someone knocked on his door.

"Come in."

Hat in hand, a middle-aged man dressed in black from head to toe nodded and entered.

"Father Murphy?"

"That's me." Murphy stood and extended a hand.

"My name is Timothy Evers. I've come from Kinsale. May I see you about a matter? It's quite important.

"It's about a murder!"

Murphy stood, eyeing his unknown, suddenly sinister-appearing visitor. "Have a chair, Mr. Evers."

Tenting his fingers, he asked, "Do you desire the sacrament of penance, my son?"

"Oh, no, Father!" Evers chuckled "I'm not Catholic.

"I'm not here to *confess* a murder. I'm here to *tell* you about a murder which has been revealed to me.

"It concerns you and Saint Timothy's."

Murphy caught his breath before leaning back in his chair. "Feel free to smoke, if you like," he invited. "Perhaps you'd care for coffee or tea, Mr. Evers?"

"Thank you, no, Father. I'm a member of the Temple of the Augury in Kinsale. You may have heard of us. We are forbidden the use of stimulants which cloud the reception of visions.

"Visions?" Murphy reached for his pipe.

"Yes, Father. Visions. Just like Saint Paul had on his way to Damascus."

Not taking his eyes off the man, Murphy began polishing his glasses. "Please tell me about your vision of a murder at Saint Timothy's."

Evers leaned forward, voice resonating with tension. "I received the first vision night before last. Then it recurred last night, assuring me that it wasn't just a passing dream.

"I am merely the messenger." Evers clenched his hands. "I cannot advise you what actions you should take to avoid this calamity. That's entirely up to you."

"Please continue, Mr. Evers."

"I was deeply asleep when an image appeared to me. The image was of your church ablaze. Fire erupted out every window and reached as high as the spire."

"And you're certain that the church was Saint Timothy's?"

"I saw a church sign. It was identical to the one at the front door which I passed on my way inside just now."

Evers' words came quicker "As I said, I saw this vision on two consecutive nights. So I hurried here today to warn you. You must take immediate action to prevent the loss of life and your church."

Murphy nodded. "I appreciate your coming here to share your vision, Mr. Evers. Ah…you mentioned a murder as well as a fire?"

Evers slowly arose from the chair. "I'd never seen you before today, Father, but I recognized you as soon as I entered this office."

He crossed his arms over his breast. Murphy couldn't help but stare.

"I saw *your* motionless body on the floor before the altar of *this* church!"

FOUR

Darkness hid the couple's activity at the river; they weren't fishing as they pretended. A silent witness was an unattended fishing pole stuck in the sand beside them.

"Have a shot," he urged. "It'll take the chill off ya."

"This is crazy," she raised the bottle to her lips "You've been watching too many spy shows on the TV. Instead, we should be cozy in a nice, warm bar somewhere."

"And be seen together by every gossip in Mallow?"

She raised her voice before he could shush her. "And why not? Are you ashamed to be seen with me? You aren't the only salmon in the Shannon! I can certainly catch another one…and quick!"

He pinched her arm and she yelped with pain.

"Quiet now," he cautioned. "You'll not be finding another man with a plan to give you so much easy money."

She struggled to free herself. "You hurt me again and you can shove your fancy plan up you-know-where!"

"Shush! A little patience is going to net you so much money you can't carry it all to the Bank of Ireland by yourself!"

"Trust me," he finished the bottle and threw it into the river.

She stood. "Trust you? Chum, I was in nappies the first time I heard that lie! I'm going home!

"And you'd better not follow me or I'll tell the *Garda*!"

Briskly, without looking back, she walked away. Once she was gone, he whispered to himself. "That would be a death wish, my love."

Mrs. Casey insisted on making him a 'hearty Irish breakfast' of eggs, rashers, blood sausage and toast with jam.

Murphy raised his hands. "Thank you, Mrs. Casey. Didn't I warn you just yesterday about spoiling me?"

Smiling, she said *sotto voce*, "The man looks a scarecrow since his return. My job is to restore him to good health. Praise God!"

In a moment, she returned from the kitchen with a pot of coffee.

"Fetch another cup," he urged. "Sit down and tell me what's really been happening here since I left last week."

She stared at him in surprise. "Oh, Father! It wouldn't be seemly for me to sit down and chat with my own priest."

She gulped at the thought, holding the apron to her face.

"Oh, come now, Mrs. Casey! Get that cup and have a seat with me! There are several things I'd like your opinion on.

"Go on, now," he urged, at her stubborn look. "Fetch yourself a cup."

In a moment she was back, nervously taking the chair farthest from his. Carefully she cupped her hands on the table, as if in prayer.

Before she could unclasp her hands or protest, he filled both cups. "If I can't discuss *our* rectory with you, then with whom?"

"Oh, Father! Miss Norton would be more appropriate than me. She has often expressed ideas about the welfare of the parish…as well as concern about your own health and well being."

Murphy began filling his pipe. "Then, next time we must ask her to join us."

"She's a bright young woman, Father. Did you know…" Casey's voice cracked.

"What is it, Mrs. Casey?"

Shutting her eyes, she began wringing her hands as if regretting she'd spoken.

"What's wrong?"

"Forgive me, Father. I had an unworthy thought about Miss Norton."

He laid the pipe in an ash tray. "You'll feel better if you relinquish the thought, whatever it was."

Eyes still shut, Casey blurted. "She has a photo of you in her room upstairs!"

"Dear Mrs. Casey. After twelve months in Afghanistan with a thousand young soldiers, nothing surprises me.

"I consider myself very fortunate that she's our administrator."

"And attractive, too," Mrs. Casey added, still ignoring her coffee.

"Ah, yes," Murphy admitted, holding a match to the pipe.

Clearing his throat, Murphy reverted to yesterday's worry. "The item I wanted to discuss with you is the security of Saint Timothy's." He blew smoke away from the table.

She frowned. "Security? What do you mean, Father?"

"Have you noticed any strangers in or around the church yard?""

"No, Father. What might a stranger be wanting here?"

"Good question, but remember, Saint Timothy's is a historical monument of great significance to Mallow as well as the whole county. I would be derelict if something happened here on my watch. A fire, for instance."

He watched her face for a reaction. Seeing none, he continued.

"That's why I'm considering asking the fire and rescue service to inspect the church and yards for hazards. Older buildings—even holy places—often contain serious hazards."

She relaxed her hands, nodding. "I'll keep an eye out for strangers or fire risks, Father. Thank you for telling me."

"You've never mentioned your family to me. Are your relatives in Dublin well?"

Casey frowned. "Ah, they're all fine, Father. Thank you for asking."

Curious, Murphy watched her hands tremble, apparently at the mention of family.

She stood up. "Now, if you'll excuse me, Father, I'm a bit behind in preparing your lunch."

"Just a moment," Murphy remembered something. "I forgot to mention that the safety inspector found a tin of petrol in a sacristy closet. Get Amos to move it outdoors, won't you?"

With that, Mrs. Casey scurried away, to return seconds later. Embarrassed, she gathered up cups and saucers, before adding "I'd appreciate your not mentioning that photo to anyone, Father."

With a wave of his hand, he assured her. "Consider it done and thank you for the coffee."

FIVE

Minutes later, Viola knocked on the door. Musing over what Mrs. Casey had said, Murphy wondered if he was acting normally. "Come in and have a chair, Viola."

"This is timely since I have several items. Yours first."

He couldn't help but noticing the administrator wore a new frock and scarf. She took the chair opposite him, seeming a bit nervous.

Murphy looked away. "What's up?"

"The ploughing match committee asks that you be a judge on Saturday next. It begins at ten but Michael Shea asks if you could please be there a bit earlier?"

Viola's hair seemed to be styled differently than the bun she usually wore. "I'd be honored. Put it on our calendar, please."

"And Mary Canady will be here at three o'clock about those threats she claims she's received." Viola looked skeptical and touched a strand of loose hair.

"Maybe I should check with the police before she comes this afternoon. I need to see the Superintendent anyway."

Viola's eyes seemed larger. "You're going to the *Garda* station, Father? I didn't think you even knew its location."

"Like Saint Timothy, bless his memory, I must be untiring."

It was after two before Father Murphy returned from his visit with the Police Superintendent at the Mallow Police Station on Bowling Green. The Superintendent and one of his inspectors had been polite as he told them about the strange message delivered by Timothy Evers.

The policemen looked dubious as he related Evers's "vision" about a murder and fire at Saint Timothy's. They promised to research the "Temple of the Augury" in Kinsale, also to increase motor patrols around the church at night.

Murphy also asked if the station had received any complaint from Mary Canady concerning threats from an unknown person.

Inspector O'Byran escorted Murphy to the investigations division. There was a record of a phone call complaint from Canady but there had been no investigation.

Later, sitting at his desk in the rectory, Murphy remembered the police reactions to Evers's vision. "Facial reactions can be more revealing than vocal responses," he mused aloud.

His reverie was short-lived as Viola knocked, then entered with Mary Canady. He contrasted their facial reactions, one composed, the other distressed.

Viola introduced the younger female with a gesture. "Father, this is Mary Canady."

"Please have a seat, Mary. I remember you from that youth group skit you performed in the parish hall last year."

As she closed the door behind her, Viola frowned at the newcomer.

Another odd facial reaction, Murphy thought.

He reached for the buzzer to ring Mrs. Casey. "Coffee or tea, Mary?"

Despite the offer, Canady looked frightened and uneasy She shook her head on which was pinned a yellow waitress cap, the same color and material as her Coffee House uniform.

Her hands shook as she spoke in a whisper. "Father, I'm

very frightened. I'm even scared that I might have been seen coming here."

Murphy rose from his chair to sit beside her on the hard bench she had chosen. He patted her hand.

"Tell me what's wrong, Mary."

Tears began streaming down her cheeks as she suddenly turned away from Murphy. He grabbed a box of tissues from the desk and silently handed it to her. In a few minutes her crying stopped, to be replaced by dry heaves.

Finally, she was able to speak.

"I'm so ashamed, Father. And you'll think less of me if I tell you...tell you of the threats."

He handed her another tissue. "I'm here to help you, Mary, not condemn you. Let me do my job. Tell me about the threats.

"Would you be more comfortable in the confessional?"

"No, Father. I'm okay here." She blinked at the desk and bare walls through her tears

Haltingly, she began. "At first it was just telephone calls bothering me at work. I thought it was some boy playing a prank on me. Still, it didn't sound like a boy."

Rather than interrupt her flow with questions, Murphy nodded.

"He sounded like an older person. Angry! If I didn't do what he wanted, he'd tell my parents. Then he threatened to superimpose my face on a photo of a naked fat woman and put it on the internet!

"I'd be ruined, he said, then he laughed like crazy."

She paused to blow her nose. Murphy waited.

"He said it was just a game—just a friendly game. It seemed innocent at first: I was to tie my yellow work scarf around a fence post on a certain day and he'll stick a 10 euro bill beneath it. Next he told me to dye my hair red, for a 20 euro bill stuck in my mail slot.

"I needed the money, so I did it.

"Two days ago, he said I must leave the Coffee House back door unbolted when I quit shift. I told him no, I wouldn't do that."

Sniffling began again. "If I didn't do it, he said he would kill Beany, my dog.

"Guess what?" Tears began again as she hid her face in both hands.

"What?" Murphy complied.

"Beanie is gone! I checked the animal catch, even put a lost dog ad in the paper.

"Nothing. Beanie's still gone…or dead!"

Murphy passed her a cup of tea from the tray Mrs. Casey just delivered.

"Did you tell your parents?"

"No, Father, and I'm praying that you won't either. Please, Father! They'll say I'm covering up my flirting with an older man."

"But you telephoned a complaint to the police?"

"I did, Father. They didn't say so, but I feel they think I'm making it all up. I need help, Father," she began crying again. "What shall I do?

"The next time it may be me who disappears…like poor Beanie!"

Murphy resisted the temptation to fill his pipe. "Could this man be one of your customers at the Coffee House? Someone who acts peculiarly toward you? Perhaps a secret admirer or a stalker?"

"I've thought and thought and thought about that, but no one acts strange. What can I do?" she wailed.

"Can you take a vacation from your job?"

"What good would that do?"

"If he's one of your customers, maybe he'll stop if you're absent for awhile."

"I can't afford to miss work, Father," her eyes filled again. "My mum and dad depend on my salary."

This time Murphy didn't hesitate. He reached for his pipe, mind racing.

"When and what day were you to leave the back door of the Coffee House unlocked?"

"Tuesday is our slowest night. I was supposed to unbolt the door on Tuesday as I left."

Murphy set down the pipe and grasped Mary's hand.

"First, join me in a prayer for your safety. Then I'm going to the police station with a idea how we might end those threats. End them by catching the low life distressing you!

"As Paul told Timothy, the namesake of our church, you must 'Have faith and love.'"

Mary agreed to come by after work the next day.

SIX

The sun shone so brightly against the eastern, whitewashed wall of John Long's tavern that Patrick Davis had to shield his eyes from the glare. Once adjusted to the bar's dimness, he asked the kitchen for a cup of tea which he set down on his favorite table farthest from the red front door.

It was the same table used by George Bailey, John Reilly and himself after the vestry meeting. That's where he suggested the three of them plan how to get bossy old Maude Connor out of the vestry.

Patrick stretched his arms and studied the Gaelic motto painted above the long mirror over the bar. "*Gluais faicilleach le cupan lan*," he read aloud. It fitted his mood and plan exactly.

"Go careful with a full cup," he repeated, then ordered three pints for himself and the two chums he expected at any moment.

"Where are those two?" He glanced out the front window, wondering their reactions to his idea about Maude. George Bailey had compared the difficulty of their task with walking on water.

"It won't be that hard gettin' rid of her," Patrick assured himself. Not when a businessman as successful as himself was on the job, he added to himself.

The round of drinks was carried to the table by Sean, the bartender. How could dubious Bailey or timid Reilly object to his plan while raising a free pint in their fists?

Pints purchased by the largesse of Patrick Davis, civic-minded entrepreneur and community leader?

The big red door banged open and Reilly entered, followed by Bailey.

"Welcome, welcome, gentlemen!" Patrick rose to greet them with a handshake and thump on the back.

Patrick gestured to the three glasses. "I'd about given up on the two of you. Then I'd have to quaff these lovely bumps by myself!

"Sit down, both of you. How's your weekend sale of fine ladies' millinery going, George? I saw your ad in the paper."

Bailey raised his pint. "Thank you, kindly, Patrick. And thanks to your wife and her friends, we almost sold out. Today I had to reorder blouses and bags from Dublin."

John Reilly also lifted his pint to Davis. "Thanks, Patrick. And thanks to you, too, George."

George set down his drink, "What am I being thanked for, Johnnie?"

Reilly beamed. "Thank goodness my wife didn't hear about your sale. If she had, I wouldn't be able to pay for the next round."

With that, the three grinned at each other as Sean delivered them fresh drinks.

Smacking his lips, Bailey set down his half-empty glass. "What's up, Patrick? Is the market taking a dive and you need our financial advice?

"We're glad to give it!" He slapped Reilly's back. "Right, John?"

"My financial advice isn't worth a pinch of salt," Reilly responded, wiping foam from his chin.

Davis leaned forward. "I've got an idea, lads."

"How to get Maud out of the vestry so we can get

something accomplished?" Bailey motioned to the bartender for more drinks.

Sighing, Reilly sat back in his chair. "Well, let's hear it, Patrick."

"Here's a thought, gents." He looked at Bailey, then Reilly. "What's the biggest social event in our parish?"

"The Mallow Stakes!" boomed George. "The race track!"

"No, man," Patrick held up both hands. "That's nothing to do with the parish. That's the town and county."

Not to be outdone, John excitedly lifted a hand. "I know! The Ladies' Altar Guild gala!"

"No, no. Pour on the imagination, gents!"

"The Young Peoples' Club?"

"More imagination!" repeated Patrick.

"The old priory dances, like at Ballybeg. That's plenty religious and lively!"

"Not bad," Patrick conceded. "What I had in mind is the celebration of the anniversary of Mallow Castle."

Pleased with himself, Patrick paused to crack his knuckles. "You see, Mallow Castle is important to us both as a religious and historical symbol. The celebration of its 500th anniversary should be the biggest event of the year, maybe in our lifetime."

George looked unconvinced. "Granted. But how do we elbow Maude out of the vestry and into planning for the big castle celebration?"

"Someone mentioned getting Father Murphy involved," John remembered. "Wasn't it you, Patrick?

Patrick only shrugged in reply as John continued. "If Father asked her to represent Saint Timothy's in planning for this anniversary, she'd have to accept. Wouldn't she?"

"Damn right," George cackled, slamming his fist on the table, upsetting his own pint.

By the time more pints had been emptied, the three men were more than chums. They were brothers, merrily banded together by a common, most worthy cause.

George stopped the hilarity by pursing his lips and asking, "How do we go about it?"

"Any thoughts, John?"

"Invite a representative of the antiquities council to meet with the vestry, Maude included of course…"

Before John could finish, Patrick completed the thought. "To emphasize the grandness of the anniversary and the heavy responsibility of the *chairperson* presently being sought. That individual would have to be a distinguished citizen of fair Mallow, who is known, respected and renowned by all."

"Here! Here!" George chanted.

"Father!" Unsteadily, John rose from the table and lifted his hand as if to make a motion to an imaginary Father Murphy presiding over an equally imaginary vestry meeting in the John Long tavern.

"It would be most fitting," he continued after a hiccup, "if a distinguished and well-known member of Saint Timothy's vestry were chosen. Well, we have such an outstanding individual serving with us on the vestry right now.

"I move we elect Mrs. Maude Connor as the *chairperson* of Mallow Castle's 500th Anniversary Celebration committee!"

Also jumping to his feet, Patrick cried, "Father, I second and move we elect Mrs. Connor by acclamation!"

Numbed by the ales and their planning acumen, the three men resumed their seats.

Patrick rapped on the rough table with his knuckles. "It goes without saying, men, that the *chairperson* must be permanently excused from the vestry because of her awesome new responsibilities."

No voice vote was needed. Already, the three men headed out the door, arm-in-arm.

SEVEN

It was a particularly dark Tuesday night. Father Murphy failed to see the kerb and loudly stubbed a black brogan against it. Biting his lip, he refused a swear word.

"Shuss!" another darkened figure, this one in police uniform, grabbed his arm and admonished him. "Be quiet! Who are you and what's your business here at this late hour?"

Murphy sat on the offending kerb, rubbing his injury, looking up at his accuser.

"Daniel Leary?"

"Father?" The policeman's tone immediately softened.

"You shouldn't be here, Father. This is a police operation. You must leave immediately for your own safety."

A third figure joined the discussion. "Quiet, you two," whispered Inspector O'Bryan, peering at them through thick glasses.

"Oh, no!" The inspector exploded, "Why are you here, Father? This is not a parish games night!"

Murphy held a finger to his lips, hoping it might slow the questions.

The priest broke the momentary silence with a whisper. "Inspector, I brought this problem to you, now I must see it through on the behalf of my threatened parishioner."

Inspector O'Bryan moaned. "If the Superintendent finds out you were here—and in the line of fire—I'll be walking patrol starting Monday.

"Or polishing a chair with my backside at some headquarters, waiting early retirement."

Murphy patted O'Bryan's shoulder. "There's a simple solution, Inspector.

"We won't tell the Superintendent. Right, Daniel?"

Constable Leary grinned. "Right, Father."

"At least get into this portal, Father. Please." The inspector urged Murphy into a darkened doorway.

"You're safer here." Then, to Leary, "Keep an eye on that back door, Constable."

Murphy leaned toward the Inspector's ear. "Have you men inside the Coffee House?"

Exasperated, O'Bryan whispered back. "Yes, Father. Three men."

Murphy peered into the other's face. "Are they armed?"

"Yes, Father. And three more men outside, counting Constable Leary, watching to see if anyone enters that unlocked back door."

Murphy was pleased. It was just as he'd suggested to the Superintendent at the *Garda* station. "Good work, Inspector."

Mollified, they stood in the portal, listening, shivering and waiting.

Overhead, scattered clouds hid the pale stars glistening in the Munster skies. Winds from the south intermittently howled, adding to the overall gloom. The streets around the Coffee House appeared deserted despite the hidden, hardly-breathing, thoroughly chilled policemen.

O'Bryan crouched in the doorway. Father Murphy, tired of standing, decided to squat beside him. O'Bryan passed the priest a dark handkerchief.

"At least cover that white collar, Father. It must be visible for several blocks."

Murphy nodded thanks and tied the handkerchief loosely around his neck.

O'Bryan's black plastic earpiece emitted a low one. The inspector listened carefully and shook his head.

"Nothing," he mouthed at Murphy.

It was two a.m., an hour later, when O'Bryan hissed. "Satisfied with your whirligig idea, Father? I'm calling this off. I've got the entire station out here drawing overtime.

"Besides," O'Bryan blew his nose, "that Mary Canady may not have gotten the message to whoever told her to leave the door unbolted."

"Sure she did," Murphy quickly assured him. "She told me so herself just hours ago. Let's stay at least until three. You and your men will probably prevent a robbery. Think how pleased your Super will be."

O'Bryan expelled his breath. "Just as a favor to you, Father, we'll stay until three."

With that the two men resumed seats in the doorway, gathering collars closer against the morning fog.

Another half-hour passed when Constable Leary approached their doorway. "They're here, Inspector!" he whispered huskily.

O'Bryan had been dozing. He sat up straight. "What?"

Leary pointed. "I just saw two figures go in the backdoor."

"Perhaps you should alert your men inside?" Murphy suggested.

O'Bryan grabbed his radio and relayed the alert, "I would have done that without your telling me, Father," he said reproachfully. "I was awake the whole time."

"Let's go, Constable," O'Bryan ordered. "We'll hit them from front and back."

Without invitation, Father Murphy followed before the inspector noticed or could object.

Inside the Coffee House, there were sounds of cursing and broken glasses as the policemen inside tried to subdue two intruders dressed in dark clothing.

"I've got one!" crowed one policeman. "A female!"

"There goes the other one! Stop him! He's heading out the front!"

A man was already outside on the street and running like an All-Ireland athlete toward the river.

"After him, men!" O'Bryan screeched. He watched the chase for a moment before turning to the female already cuffed beside Leary.

She wore navy sweater and dark trousers. Breathing heavily, she bared her teeth and angrily tossed her red braids as she glared at O'Bryan.

"What's your name, girl?"

"I demand a lawyer!"

"And you'll get one. Now what's your name?"

"No purse, no ID," Leahy answered O'Bryan's look.

"You're under arrest for breaking and entering and resisting arrest. Now what's your name?" he repeated.

She compressed her lips as if to spit but said nothing.

"Plus refusing to identify yourself to law enforcement. Congratulations, you just graduated from our gaol to Limerick Prison!

"We're off to the station, Father. Afraid I can't invite you to go with us."

Murphy pursed his lips. "And why not? In Afghanistan,

we planned an ambush, conducted, then critiqued it. I'd like to be present."

"No, Father, the Superintendent would have a fit.

"Let's move, Constable," he motioned to the car pulling up to the kerb. "Hopefully the lads have run the other suspect to ground by now.

"Meanwhile, I'm telephoning the owner and posting a man to secure the Coffee House until the owner arrives."

As the female prisoner was being pushed into the back seat, she eyed Father Murphy's now exposed white collar.

"You'll see my chum before the police will, Mr. Dog Collar. You'll pay a high price for helping this lot! And so will that prissy Canady bitch!"

EIGHT

"Telephone for you, Father," Viola called him the next morning after morning prayers.

Murphy shifted the just-started homily notes on his littered desk to pick up the telephone. "Maybe it's someone about my missing old bicycle?"

"Don't think so," she responded. "It's Inspector O'Bryan calling."

"Good morning, Inspector. Father Murphy here."

"Good morning, Father," the inspector sounded drowsy. "Wish I could say we've jailed that other robber, but he got clean away from my lads. They lost him somewhere around Bridewell Lane."

"Do we know his name?"

"Not yet, Father, but we're working on that. The Superintendent asked me to call to express his gratitude for your assistance in helping the force prevent that robbery."

Murphy grinned, imagining the Superintendent's chagrin at acknowledging any unofficial help, especially from Saint Timothy's.

"Please thank the Superintendent for his kind words. What about the identity of that young girl?"

"She has a record under the name of Maureen Hanrihan. Not sure if that's her real name. She used to live in Grove Gardens."

Murphy fiddled with a pencil. "Since she threatened my parishioner, could you provide Mary Canady some security?"

"We're stretched thin but we've alerted foot and motor patrols to keep an eye on young Miss Canady."

O'Bryan hesitated. "I imagine you're concerned about your own safety, Father. Sounds like the girl's chum—as she called him—may target you for reprisal."

"I'm amply protected by Saint Timothy as well as my housekeeper. Mrs. Casey. She keeps a stout shillelagh beside her broom."

O'Bryan chuckled. "Just in case, our patrols will watch out for you, too, Father."

"Thanks, Inspector, not to worry. Any news on that other Timothy? I mean Timothy Evers of Kinsale and his temple?"

Murphy could hear O'Bryan shuffling papers. "Yes, Father. We have a report that he is the head mogul of the Temple of the Augury there. They seem to be another odd, but harmless cult. Despite the church's efforts, Father, Ireland seems to abound in them nowadays. This lot is neither anarchist nor terrorist according to the Crime and Security Branch.

"Anyway, think I'd best say a prayer for your safety now and again, Father."

Maude Connor, seated at the head of the formal dining table, cleared her throat so the housekeeper and cook standing before her could hear their instructions clearly.

"I'm planning on a private luncheon with the Father here on Tuesday."

The housekeeper and cook both held their breaths.

"Here is the menu I'd like you to prepare, Annie. You'll have to go to the greengrocers tomorrow to buy the necessary. And," she eyed the housekeeper, "the dining room, silverware and parlor must be properly prepared of course."

The housekeeper and cook, from long practice, answered in unison. "Yes, Madam."

Housekeeper Eunice raised a hand. "Just the two of you, Madam? Miss Norton will not be accompanying the Father!"

"Goodness, no! What an idea!"

The housekeeper adjusted her frame glasses defensively. "Her being the parish administrator and all, she usually accompanies Father Murphy, Madam."

Maud set down her tea cup so hard, it sounded like a pistol shot. The housekeeper and cook paled.

"She is not invited, is that clear?"

"Yes, Madam."

Staring at the carpeting, they withdrew quickly.

Murphy paused at his office door, looking over his shoulder. "You're not coming with me?"

"No, Father, not invited. I'll be here praying that you return unscathed from your luncheon with 'Her Ladyship.'"

Despite himself, Murphy grinned. "None of that now, Viola. I'm sure Mrs. Connor has many virtues we can't yet fathom."

As he was adjusting his big black hat, she rushed to him. "Here, Father. You'd better be taking pencil and paper."

He eyed her, cocking his head with the unasked question.

"Mrs. Connor may be giving you a few tasks, Father. You'll need to make note of them."

Outside, Murphy wheeled his recently-recovered 'High Nelly' bicycle out of the yard and pedaled off. Soon he was in front of the Connor large red-brick residence, locally referred to as the 'Manor House.' He was met at the door.

"Good day, Eunice," he responded to the housekeeper's welcome. "I've come calling on Mrs. Connor."

"Yes, this way, Father. Mrs. Connor is receiving you in the high parlor."

Seated on a slightly raised dais, Connor rose as Murphy entered. "So good of you to come, Father. I'm certain to be disrupting your busy schedule on such short notice. I must apologize."

She gestured to chairs. "I've known many rectors of Saint Timothy's, Father, and they were invariably hungry. I hope my little menu today will be appealing and that you'll return here to sample many others."

Murphy nodded. "Meals at the manse tend to be plain and hardy. It was very kind of you to invite me for a visit today."

"Would you care for a small glass of port before lunch, Father?"

"Only if you are having one, Maude." He used her baptismal name to avoid repeating 'Mrs. Connor, Mrs. Connor' throughout the visit. He looked about, admiring the room.

"Your parlor is very impressive. It reminds me of the Bishop's Palace."

She tinkled a small bell for Eunice to serve the port. "It's been our home for generations, Father. You know my family has been here since the Normans."

He did know, having heard her last sentence many times.

As he took a glass of port, he wondered why he was invited today, his first. Was Viola right about Connor's having an agenda other than social?

He patted a side pocket for the pencil and paper stuck there by Viola. Would the reason for this luncheon become apparent before or after the soup course?"

It came sooner than that. As he raised his glass to Maude, she leaned forward as if to share a secret. "To tell the truth…"

Murphy smiled at the phrase, having heard it so often in the confessional.

"Father, I hope to ask your counsel on several suggestions for our vestry."

They set down their empty glasses and she led him into a dining room even more opulent than the parlor. The housekeeper already held a chair for Mrs. Connor so Murphy took the seat opposite.

The four course luncheon was a feast for Murphy. Mrs. Casey, his housekeeper, prepared sparse but filling meals. Breakfast was usually coffee, toast and oatmeal. Lunch was a thin barley or rice soup. Dinner consisted of leftovers from the previous day plus cabbage or potatoes and, maybe, a pudding.

Murphy declined a second cup of coffee while edging his chair away from the table, trying to position pencil and paper in his lap.

"Father, you are smiling like never before!" Connor exclaimed. "What is it?"

"Mrs. Connor," he addressed her formally. "That was the finest lunch I've ever enjoyed. It was splendid! That bread and butter pudding was exceptional. Thank you.

"I'm afraid Saint Timothy's can never reciprocate with a meal as grand as this."

He folded his napkin. "You spoke of the vestry, which

I believe you've been a leading member of for going-on ten years?"

Maude Connor twisted her napkin, pleased with his memory. She might even give her staff a surprise, half-day off some week.

'Got him!' she thought. 'Now is the time to capitalize!'

"I do have an idea," she confessed. "I'd like to present you a possible worthy project for our vestry to initiate. Under your leadership, it might be of tremendous benefit to Saint Timothy's, thus to our city."

Murphy edged his paper and pencil into position, mentally blessing Viola.

"Yes?"

"Father, I'm certain that in your position as not only a community but county leader, you are concerned with the rising crime rate in our city."

"I'm unaware of any raging crime in our midst. I'll have to ask the police for particulars." Murphy wrote O'Bryan's name on his paper.

"Surely you know, Father, that many such crimes are unreported, particularly those occurring in our public parks at night."

His expression blank, Murphy already guessed Connor's objective.

"Father, I won't speak of the terrible things I've been told which happen in our parks after hours. It would be unseemly of me to express them to you. Were I to speak frankly, your opinion of me must suffer. I will leave their descriptions to others."

"I'll certainly inquire." Pencil posed over paper, innocently he asked. "I presume you have a solution in mind?"

"Under your leadership," Connor began reciting the words she practiced last night, "the vestry might consider appealing to the city council to close the parks during the hours of darkness. That might remedy the problem."

"I see." He quietly folded and began to replace the paper in a coat pocket.

She stayed his action. "There is one more subject about which I'd appreciate your advice, Father."

He nodded. "Please continue."

"It's about the membership of our vestry. Several members have been there for many years. Just as an example, Mrs. Kennedy has served on the vestry for over twenty years. Several other members might appreciate the opportunity to retire. Fresh minds and modern attitudes would revitalize our somnolent vestry.

"Perhaps you might consider calling for a new election of members?"

His first thought was 'What's old Mrs. Kennedy done to offend?' Instead he countered, "We have a brand new, newly-elected member in John Reilly."

She pursed her lips. "So new, he was absent from our last meeting, Father. But he was able to meet later in the bar with two other vestry members, I'm told."

"I'll pray for guidance, Mrs. Connor. Thank you again for not only a marvelous luncheon but for sharing your concerns about the vestry and our community." He rose from the table.

"It was my pleasure to have you visit Manor House, Father," she moved to the door. "Before I forget, my cook heard you liked her pudding, so she jotted down her recipe. Perhaps you'd like it for your cook in the manse."

Once on his bicycle and pedaling back to Saint Timothy's, Murphy yelped, "Preserve me!" and speeded up, barely missing a dog scratching in the street.

Proud of her planned presentation, Maude Connor watched Father Murphy pedal away on his ancient bicycle. Once he was out of sight, she rang the little bell for Eunice.

"Bushmills and ice in a large glass," she instructed, settling in a leather cushion chair. Once Eunice brought the drink and departed, Connor sipped the whiskey, mentally reviewing her next moves.

"First," she murmured so she couldn't be overheard, "I'll persuade the Father and vestry to petition our town council to restrict the operating hours of all bars and public houses.

"That'll be difficult," she admitted, "but we can publicize the increasing number of drunks being arrested by police in the evenings. If the village of Macroom did it, so can the city of Mallow!" She held one finger aloft.

"Women should be prohibited from wearing those horrid bikinis in public pools. Also, no more of those revealing 'short-shorts.'" She raised a second finger accompanied by a larger sip of Bushmills.

Once the glass was empty, she closed her eyes for a short nap, dreaming of other changes she had in mind.

NINE

That afternoon Father Murphy sat on a bench overlooking the children's playground. A dozen youngsters, ages six to ten, played boisterously on the slides, swings and merry-go-rounds. He had just finished a weekly inquirers' class for their mothers. Murphy's presentation ended and mothers were assembling their noisy offspring for the return home.

Shading her eyes, Viola Norton, carrying a cell phone, approached the bench where he sat, enjoying the childrens' antics.

"Join you, Father?"

"Please do. Aren't they amazing?"

"The children or the mothers, Father?"

"Both. I saw you admiring the young ones as you came across the yard. Hope to have children of your own?"

Smiling, she nodded. "Yes, Father. Some day. When I find that perfect man."

Her response troubled him. "There is only one perfect man, Viola."

She looked at him steadily. "I know, Father. But I heard you tell the mothers just now that faith and hope will always prevail."

"Commit your needs to prayer and the results will amaze you."

She blushed, disrupting her long look at Murphy. "How was your luncheon with Maude Connor, Father?"

He chuckled. "Thank you for the pencil and paper you were wise enough to tuck into my coat. How did you possibly know she'd unload some favorite chores on unsuspecting me?"

Before she could answer, her cell phone buzzed. She answered, passing it to him. "For you, Father. It's that Inspector O'Bryan."

Viola felt another blush as she passed the phone into his hand.

"Father Murphy here. I'm imagining that you have that male robber in custody?"

O'Bryan swallowed noisily. "No, Father. I'm the messenger of bad news. Remember that young girl we arrested?"

"Of course," Murphy paused. "I hope she didn't harm herself in her cell?"

O'Bryan wheezed. "No, Father. She escaped! She was being transported to the Limerick Prison, awaiting trial. On the way, she managed to overturn our vehicle and escape."

Murphy closed his eyes. "That's terrible! Anyone injured?"

O'Bryan sounded deflated by his own news. "Our guard/driver was trapped beneath the vehicle, unconscious but, hopefully, with only minor injuries. That's the only bright aspect of my report, Father."

"Great that he wasn't seriously injured! I should visit him in the hospital."

"He's being checked but appears to be healthy despite an aching head. Unfortunately, there's more.

"The girl's name is Aileen Hannrihan, although she goes by the nickname of Cherie. She's missing and probably on the way to rejoin the other robber, the one she called her chum."

"I remember. So you're calling to alert me that they soon may be on their way to Mallow to possibly harm someone?"

"Right, Father. It gets worse. That Cherie took the service

pistol of the unconscious guard/driver. So now we must presume the pair is armed and more dangerous than before!

"We're borrowing policemen from other stations so we can double our coverage of Mary Canady, you and Saint Timothy's, Father.

"The Superintendent regrets this dangerous situation. He urges you to be alert and take the utmost care. If something seems amiss, call me immediately."

Murphy returned the phone to an ashen Viola who heard the conversation.

He stood and offered a hand to help her up. "Let's go to the kitchen for a hot cup of coffee with Mrs. Casey. We must tell her and Amos about the possible appearance of Cherie and her partner at Saint Timothy's."

Viola touched his shoulder. "You're their obvious target, Father. Perhaps you should visit the diocese for a few days, just until that pair is caught."

Amused, Murphy looked at her. "Thank you for your concern, but I don't think Saint Timothy would hide, do you?"

Inspector O'Bryan took special care with his uniform earlier that day. He buffed his shoes, polished brass, even slicked down an unruly lock of hair. He stood for a moment before knocking at the Super's door.

"Enter." As expected, the command sounded angry.

O'Bryan neither expected nor received an invitation to sit in the chair opposite the Superintendent's desk. He saluted smartly.

"You look knackered, Inspector," was his superior's dry observation.

Before O'Bryan could respond, the Superintendent snapped, "Report."

"Sir, I arranged a vehicle and driver to transport female prisoner Hannrihan to the Limerick Prison for confinement whist awaiting trial…"

"Charges?"

O'Bryan deftly recited the charges without notes. "Breaking and entering, resisting arrest, assault of a police officer and refusing to identify self."

"Was the prisoner cuffed?"

"Yes, sir. Plasticuffs were used due to the small size of the prisoner's wrists."

"And?'

The inspector took a deep breath. "Prisoner was searched by a matron, put aboard the vehicle and departed here at 0700 hours, sir."

"Did you inspect the driver and guard, Inspector?"

Beginning to perspire, O'Bryan caught another breath. "Only one constable was available at that time, Superintendent. Yes, sir. I inspected Constable Faraday, his vehicle and firearm and found all satisfactory."

"What do standard operating procedures require?"

O'Bryan stared straight ahead. "Normally another constable is required, sir. In view of the size and …ah… gender of the prisoner, I thought one constable could serve as driver and guard."

The Superintendent slammed his baton on the desk. "Inexcusable, Inspector!"

"Yes, sir."

"Poor judgement! And from a senior police officer!"

"No excuse, sir."

"Continue."

O'Bryan took another breath. "Approximately ten kilometers north of Mallow, sir, is a high embankment over which the E203 highway passes. At that point, the prisoner claimed she was about vomit. While the driver's attention was diverted, the prisoner grabbed the steering wheel and jerked it to the side. The vehicle tumbled down the embankment and crashed, knocking the driver unconscious. The prisoner managed to extricate herself from the vehicle and escape."

The Superintendent's eyes narrowed into slits. "And what did your small female prisoner escape with?"

Apoplectic, O'Bryan answered. "She took the unconscious constable's service pistol, sir. We began an immediate search for the prisoner once the accident was reported."

"And?"

"As yet, we have not located or captured the prisoner. The injured constable is being treated at the Mallow Medical Center. His condition is reported to be stable, sir."

The Superintendent stood behind his desk and pointed his baton at O'Bryan. "I hold you personally responsible for the quick recapture," he repeated, "recapture of that prisoner.

"Report to me when you have completed that assignment. Later I'll evaluate your performance and judgment in this sad affair."

"Yes, sir." He saluted, did a snappy about face and quietly closed the door behind him.

There he breathed deeply again.

"Here Sean, here!" The John Long bar already was crowded and noisy by eleven that morning. Men poured through the red front door, sat in vacant chairs and unwrapped thick sandwiches. To be palatable, sandwiches were best consumed with large amounts of liquids, preferably John Long's lager, stout or ale.

"Three pints here, Sean!" George Bailey yelled all the louder to be heard by the busy bartender behind the counter. Bailey, John Reilly and Pat Davis rushed to their favorite table and grabbed chairs. Happy to find their usual seats, they sat down, contented to watch the midday hubbub about them.

"How'd you get by your missus?" Davis squinted at Reilly who usually walked the several miles into Mallow.

"Said I was coming to town to look for hybrid seed for planting this spring," Reilly winked.

Bailey joined the game. "And did you find any?"

"No," Reilly grinned. "I'll go home this afternoon with neither seed nor silver in my pocket."

"Well, I'm buying this round," Bailey declared, scratching his nose. "Tell me, Mr. Chairman," he turned to Davis. "What's the reason for this board meeting?"

"We're here to plan…" Davis began.

"The ouster…" Bailey continued, clinking his pint against the others.

"Of 'Her Ladyship' from the parish vestry," Reilly finished.

"Exactly!" Davis raised and clasped his hands like a boxer. "Here's how we might tackle the task.

"Who's the vestry member most respected by Father Murphy?"

"Surely not 'Her Ladyship.' Reilly frowned at his pint.

"Bad guess," Bailey chided him. "Has to be one of the ladies: Viola, his administrator; Joyce, our recorder; or old Mrs. Kennedy."

"Agree," Davis did a thumbs up. "Has to be the venerable Mrs. Kennedy. She's known the Father since he was a boy. I say we go to see her and present our case. Convince her that Connor would be the ideal chairperson of the Castle anniversary effort…"

It was Reilly's time to finish the thought. "Leaving the vestry to its sacred business with fresh focus."

"Sounds like a politician, doesn't he?" Davis elbowed Bailey. "And he claims to be a farmer!

"We win Mrs. Kennedy and she sells the idea to Father Murphy!"

An exuberant Davis stood, holding up three fingers. "Three pints, Sean! Three more, please."

TEN

After catechism class, Viola rapped on Murphy's door and poked her head inside. He looked up from his breviary and nodded.

"Father, Marie Sullivan and Ron Calhoun are here for marriage counseling. Remember you agreed to see them whenever it was convenient for them?"

"I remember. Show them in, please."

"And Father…"

He smiled at her pensive look. "Yes?"

"I'd like a minute with you whenever possible. Just a minute will do."

The marriage counseling lasted for over two hours. As the happy couple departed, Viola reappeared at the door.

Murphy waved. "Come in, come in. Have a chair."

He pointed at a bottle of wine which the aspiring to-be-weds presented him.

"It must have been a success. They want to be married here next month. They even left us a bottle of wine. I just happen to have two glasses here which Mrs. Casey must have overlooked."

Viola took a seat, shaking her head. "Mrs. Casey didn't overlook them, Father. She must have known about your gift. As the old folks say, she 'has the sight.' She can even recite a list of my few possessions."

Murphy removed the cork and filled their glasses, handing her one. He remembered Mrs. Casey's acuity. She knew Viola kept his photograph in her room.

She began dubiously. "Is wine at mid afternoon all right, Father?"

He raised his glass. "Paul advised our Timothy that a little wine was good for his stomach. Paul's wisdom applies to us as well. Cheers."

He slapped himself on the forehead. "We should have invited Mrs. Casey and Amos, too."

Finishing his glass and setting it down, he raised eyebrows, questioning.

She responded to his look. "That phone call from Inspector O'Bryan interrupted your sharing with me what happened at Maude Connor's lunch."

Murphy packed his pipe and looked at Viola expectantly.

"Certainly, Father. This is your office. Smoke whenever you like."

He lit the pipe, swiveling his chair so she wouldn't face the smoke. "She talked about two changes she wants...er...recommends.

"First, Maude thinks our vestry should become an agent for change. She wants the vestry to present proposals to the city council in the name of Saint Timothy's. Of course the council may or may not enact the change.

"Her top item is to close our public parks during the hours of darkness. She says the purpose is to lower the incidence of crime—or whatever—occurring in the parks after hours."

Murphy rotated his chair to face her. "What are your thoughts?"

Viola leaned forward. "Maybe it's the wine talking, Father, but I dislike the idea of our vestry—our church—assuming a civic role.

"I don't know what happens in parks after dark. Other

than bars and restaurants, young couples have few places to meet after work. And I imagine lots of families take their children there to play if there's no yard or garden at home."

Murphy nodded. "Good points. Like you, I'm unaware that there's crime or violence in the parks. Maybe there's no real problem, other than in Maude's mind."

"Forgive me, Father, if I'm being critical of another."

He tamped out the pipe. "I appreciate your thoughts, Viola." Noting her blush, he continued. "There's more. The parks aren't her only concern."

Murphy answered her raised eyebrows. "The vestry, too."

Viola held her breath. "Tell me, Father. I can't imagine what it is unless she wants more people on the vestry to perform those new responsibilities."

He chuckled. "You must have 'the sight', too, Viola. She wants new vestry elections to fill the vacancies created by 'retiring' our older members."

"Like Mrs. Kennedy, I suppose?"

"Right, again. But let's keep Maude's ideas to ourselves for the moment."

"Were I a bettor, Father, I'd wager there are lots more changes she'd like to make."

He nodded.

Viola sighed. "Well, Father, let's pray that none of them prove fatal."

ELEVEN

Murphy sat at his desk for a long time after Viola left. Something—some word—she used was so out of character for her that it triggered a submerged memory. What had she said?

He shut his eyes searching for the word.

"Fatal," he repeated. That was the word.

Suddenly he remembered a morning in Afghanistan the previous year. He was squatting on Hill 3787, the apex of Kandahar and Zabul provinces.

"Fatal," the battalion surgeon announced as he and Murphy huddled over the bloody body of Private Theodore (Teddy) Kelly of Charlie Company on a stretcher. His lower abdomen had been riddled by a rocket propelled grenade fired by the Taliban across the valley.

The doctor stood and touched Murphy's shoulder. "He felt no pain, Father. He died instantly."

Kelly, a quiet, black-haired teenager from Dublin, was the battalion's fourth casualty since occupying its current positions atop Hill 3787. He was well-liked and often shared after-Army plans for marriage and career with his priest.

Murphy felt the need for more words from the doctor. That one word—fatal—seemed terribly insufficient to announce the death of a young man who would never tip another pint, kiss a young girl, marry or delightedly bounce his child on a knee.

"Fatal," he had repeated the word while kissing and encircling his neck with the thin purple stole. Corpsmen stood nearby, respectfully doffing their camo headgear as grimy as Murphy's battle dress uniform.

He knelt beside Kelly's body and gently closed the eyelids. He repeated a favorite prayer for the dead, used so often it was memorized. After the corpsmen placed the remains in a body bag, Murphy led them to the temporary mortuary behind the aid station. He remained for a long time with Private Teddy Kelly, this time praying for Teddy's family.

That afternoon he wrote a letter to Teddy's family in Dublin, expressing not only his grief but respect and admiration of their son. Once returned to Ireland, Murphy made a point to correspond with the Kellys, even visiting them once in Dublin to hand them a photo of a grinning Teddy taken by one of his comrades.

"Father?"

Startled, Murphy looked at the paper on his desk. He had been writing a letter of condolence to the Kellys, a mirror image of the one he'd penned over a year ago on Hill 3787.

Mrs. Casey stood at the door, frowning. "Father. Are you alright? Are you ill?"

He stood, clearing his mind of the memory. "Thank you, Mrs. Casey. I'm fine."

"In that case, may I bring you a strong cup of tea, Father?"

"Yes, bless you. Bring one for you, too, please."

"Bejesus! You scared the devil outta me!"

She slapped him hard. "Don't ever do that again," she snarled.

The young man grabbed her arms and drew her close. "Shows how glad I am to have you back, Cherie."

She pushed away from him. "No thanks to you, Joe. You ran out of that coffee shop like a singed rat, leaving me behind for the police. No thanks to you, either, that I escaped from that van on the way to prison.

"If it were up to you, cocky, I'd be sitting in a cell right now while you are out getting ossified with a new feek."

He pulled her down on the pallet. "Listen, you and I are joined at the hip. With that pistol and your looks, we'll get lots of money! It'll be like feeding biscuits to a bear. We can't get enough!"

She pointed a finger in his face. "Look, rock head. My photo is all over Ireland by now. You'll have to be the unknown armed gunman, not me. I'm tired of being the wind dummy for your ideas."

He thumped his finger against her forehead. "Well, you're the tool! You told them I'd be back to even the score with that priest!"

"Take the pistol," she shoved it into his stomach. "And bring me some money by dark."

Hats in hand, John, Patrick and George rang the doorbell of the Kennedy family home on Church Street, just two blocks from Saint Timothy's. Before ringing, they had hand-brushed off coats and slicked down their hair.

"Let me do the talking," Patrick repeated. Both had already agreed Davis should be the spokesman on their short walk from the John Long bar.

The door opened and a black-uniformed woman studied them before stepping aside. "Madame is in the parlor, gentlemen. Be kind enough to wipe your feet before entering."

Sitting in an old rocking chair, Mrs. Kennedy pointed to three chairs arranged before her. "Have a seat, gentlemen."

She signaled the servant. "Tea, Annie!"

Patrick Davis began in his well-practiced business tone. "Thank you for seeing us on short notice, Mrs. Kennedy."

She leaned forward. "Skip the blather, Patrick. I reckon you're not here to cadge a free tea nor discuss the weather. What is it you want?"

Patrick managed to smile. "We're here to discuss vestry business with you, Mrs. Kennedy. We respect you as the senior member of the vestry and request your opinion on a number of matters."

Mrs. Kennedy sniffed. "Why aren't we sitting around the vestry table at the church instead of here in my home?"

George Bailey decided it was his turn to be as blunt as Kennedy. "It concerns Maude Connor trying to take over our entire program, like she did the last time."

Nudging Bailey, Davis retrieved his role as spokesman. "We know there is a prestigious position available for a person as highly qualified as Mrs. Connor, a position which will benefit Mallow as well as Cork. This most responsible position would require her absence from vestry duties for an extended period," he added with a wink.

Kennedy pursed thin lips. "And what would this prestigious position be?"

Patrick nodded at George to answer. "The chairperson for planning and organizing the 500th anniversary of Mallow Castle!"

Kennedy chuckled. "And I thought the IRA was

disbanded long ago! How do you scoundrels," she wrinkled her nose at Bailey and Davis, "propose to pluck her from our breast, so to speak?"

"We suggest you discuss it privately with the Father. With his permission, the vestry can unanimously recommend Maude as Saint Timothy's candidate for the chairperson job."

"And none too quick," she growled. "I've been told Maude wants a new vestry election. Anyone with more than ten years of service on the vestry is to be 'retired,' which includes everyone here except you, John Reilly.

"Annie!" Kennedy bawled. "Forget the tea, bring us four cold Guinness instead!"

TWELVE

"Wake up! I'm back!" He beat on her bare shoulder.

Drowsy but mad, she sat up on the mattress and demanded. "What did you get me?"

Giddy, he poured a fistful of coins into her lap. "Here's what! Am I a great provider or not?"

She sniffed, beginning to separate and count the coins. "Barely enough here to buy me a good bra. Where did you get it?"

"You'll never guess."

"Just tell me. Where?"

"I hit that coffee spot again. Same place!

"I just walked in and grabbed the money outa' the register. Got away just like before: fleet of foot! I should be in the Olympics!"

She began dressing and stuffing clothing in an old suitcase.

"What are you doing?" he demanded.

"Getting outa here before the police break down the door! Spanner! Do you think you weren't recognized and followed?"

"Calm down, calm down! The place was empty."

She paused in packing the clothing. "How did you get in?"

"I'd unlocked the back door when I was inside, like a regular customer going to the toilet. Piece of cake!

"And there's something else. Hey! Where are you going?"

She snapped the case shut and put on her cap "To my auntie, that's where, until things cool off. I'm not going to be a caught again and almost imprisoned, thanks to you."

"Wait! Remember that girl at the coffee house, that Mary something?"

Hand on knob, she paused. "So?"

"Her folks have a car. I saw it once, parked outside the Coffee House. With that car we could go anywhere, maybe take the ferry over to Liverpool! Imagine that!"

"If you get a car, you can come by my aunt's place and pick me up. If not, kiss off!"

The thin door trembled as she slammed it behind her.

Mrs. Casey was ironing Father Murphy's alb when her cell phone sounded. "Yes?"

"Father Murphy, please. Inspector O'Bryan calling."

"Father is not available," Casey's voice broke but she recovered immediately. "He's conducting a marriage. Can he call you back later?"

"A marriage!" To someone else, the speaker repeated, "lady says he's marrying someone, Inspector. Can he return your call when he's through?"

"Damn!" The inspector took the telephone. "I'll speak to her.

"Inspector O'Bryan here. Who is this?"

"Mrs. Casey, Father Murphy's housekeeper," she replied, even more nervous.

O'Bryan's tone softened. "Please ask the Father to call me at the police station. We have one of his parishioners here in custody in connection with a robbery. A Miss..." papers rustled in the background, "Mary Canady of Mallow asks for Father Murphy's assistance. She's in a bit of a jam, you see."

The parish hall was ablaze with yellow flowers as

well-wishers paraded by the just married couple, extending congratulations and best wishes. Fruit punch and apple cake were being served at the end of the receiving line by the Ladies' Guild.

Father Murphy stood nearby, hoping to discourage any alcoholic additions to the punch. Beside him stood Viola Norton. As people entered the hall, they paused to shake hands and chat with their priest and parish administrator.

Siobhain O'Toole whispered to the lady helping her ladle the punch. "Aren't they just the handsome couple? They could pass for a bride and groom, don't you think?"

The whisper was returned. "Who?"

Siobhain inclined her head. "Father and Viola standing over there, of course."

Conjecture was cut short as Mrs. Casey stepped up to Murphy with her cell phone. "Call for you, Father, from Inspector O'Bryan. Seems to be an emergency."

An hour earlier a different group gathered in the public room of the John Long's. Pat, George and John had invited the other members of the vestry for an unexpected get-together, suggested by Mrs. Kennedy.

"It'll be good practice for later when we start our after-vestry parties," George waved at the bartender. "We'll get the ladies in the habit right away. Later we'll ask the Father to come, too!"

John escorted the female members of the vestry, minus Maude Connor, into the public room to the special table they'd reserved.

Mrs. Kennedy in the lead, sat down at the head of the table in the chair offered by George. Viola, right behind her, sat down next. Joyce MacDoo, the secretary, looking around as if it were her first time in a tavern, chose the seat across from Viola.

Thumbs hooked in his vest, Patrick began. "Thank you for coming, ladies. Drinks are on the gents in celebration of this grand occasion."

Bartender Sean stood there, listening to their orders without pen or pencil. Nodding and repeating the order, he left for the bar in the next room.

"And three more pints for us, Sean," George added.

Without preliminaries, Patrick went straight to the crux. "We've asked you here, ladies, to discuss the future of our vestry. Do we prefer continuing the past practice where the good Mrs. Connor largely determines our agenda?

"Or would you prefer that the six of us sitting right here determine—with the Father's blessing of course—our vestry's future plans in the absence of Maude Connor?"

Immediately Joyce and Viola asked the question, almost in the same breath. "Where's Maude going?"

Mrs. Kennedy turned to the other ladies after clearing her throat. "We hope to persuade Maude to become the chairperson responsible for the planning of the 500th anniversary of Mallow Castle. Those important, fulltime," she emphasized, "responsibilities would preclude her presence on our vestry."

After a moment, Viola injected. "We would need the Father's approval for that."

"Yes, dear," Kennedy smiled. "As administrator, we hope you will be our strong right arm in persuading him. We'll all participate, of course."

Everyone around the table nodded vigorously.

Patrick resumed. "We're here to ask you ladies' approval of our tentative plan."

"Yes! Let's rid Maude of our vestry!" Joyce raised her tankard. "I'm all for it and overdue!"

"Second!" Viola jumped up, raising her own glass.

"All in favor?"

After fervent 'Ayes' from around the table, George signaled the bar for another round.

Mrs. Kennedy held up a manicured finger glinting with diamonds. "Now we need to plan how we broach this delicate subject with the Father. I think it important, again, that we all participate."

Everyone nodded except Patrick who raised his hand. "Mrs. Kennedy, as our senior vestry member, I suggest you be our main speaker. Father Murphy values your opinion and advice more than the rest of us combined, I wager. The rest of us will fill in the dots, so to speak."

Kennedy sat back, looking at each face. "Does that meet with your approval? I don't intend to become another domineering old lady. We already have one too many."

Agrees, all round, were accompanied by chuckles.

"Then, Viola would you please put us on the Father's schedule and inform everyone here. Except Maude, of course, who'll attend our later regular vestry meeting after the Father's decision."

Sean arrived with the new drinks and passed them around the table.

"Before I forget," Kennedy cleared her throat again, "please come by the Manor House tomorrow, Patrick, and let me practice my little speech to the Father."

"Meeting adjourned!" called Joyce, in her official voice.

THIRTEEN

A female constable led Mary Canady to the interview room where Father Murphy waited. With a nod to Murphy the constable said "I'm right outside, Father. Knock when you're through with the prisoner."

Already red-eyed and pale, Mary flinched on hearing the word "prisoner." She collapsed in the chair opposite Murphy, tears pouring down her face.

Murphy offered his handkerchief and patted her hand. "Take your time, Mary. When you're ready, tell me what happened. I've not seen the police report if there is one".

He looked around the bare room. "Would you like a drink of water?"

"No, thank you, Father," she sniffled, wringing the handkerchief in both small hands. "Thank you for coming."

"I'm concerned about you, Mary. To your credit, you helped the police thwart a robbery of the Coffee House. You're a most respected member of Saint Timothy's and I'm here to offer any assistance possible.

"Tell me why you're here, whenever you're ready."

She swallowed before again collapsing in tears. "I'm so ashamed, Father! The police came to our house at midnight and took me to jail in handcuffs. My parents think I'm a criminal! Maybe you do, too!"

"Tell me why the police arrested you, Mary. What happened?"

After a few moments, both tears and hiccups subsided. "Last night, the Coffee House was burgled, like before. But this time whoever it was got away with the money in the register. Mr. Ross must have forgotten to empty the register and lock the cash in the overnight safe. If there's much money, he takes it direct to the bank for deposit."

She acknowledged Murphy's puzzled look. "Mr. Ross said I left the backdoor unbolted. as we did before for the police that time. He accuses me of being an accessory, a member of the robbery gang!

"The police believe him, arrested me and brought me here. That's all I know, Father," she pleaded.

"Please believe me," she began sobbing again. "I had nothing to do with the robbery but Mr. Ross wants me charged and held for trial."

Murphy clasped his hands, studying her. Finally he spoke and smiled. "Let's start with your coming to work yesterday. Tell me everything that happened no matter how minor you think it. Everything," he repeated.

To provide a momentary time-out for Mary to recall details, he ran a finger between his warm neck and the tight white collar.

She began in a whisper. "I was here at 5:30 in the morning and ..."

He interrupted. "How did you get to work, Mary?"

"I walked from my folks' house. Got here at 5:30, that's when Mr. Ross likes me to open the place."

"You have a key to the front door? Back door, too?"

"Only the front door, Father. The back is kept locked except for deliveries."

"Next?"

"I turned on the lights, opened the shades—like always—and started the coffee maker and boiler for tea. Then I wiped the tables clean and set out fresh napkins."

Murphy nodded.

"By then Dick, our cook, was here to light the oven and start baking the buns and breads. Then Mr. Ross came in."

"What time did Ross and the cook arrive?"

She turned to look at the clock on the wall behind her. Nodding, she said "It must have been 6:00. We have several customers who always come by 6:00 for their coffee and sweet buns."

"Did Ross and the cook seem normal to you? Did they go about their usual duties?"

"Oh, yes, Father. Just like always."

"Go on, please."

"Well," she hesitated. "it was the usual morning. Business picked up a bit by noon, what with lunch and all."

"Were any of the customers new? Did you know them all?"

"Mostly the same rowdy bunch of men."

"Does Mr. Ross handle the cash register all day or do you help him at times?"

She pursed her lips, remembering. "We weren't real busy. He did the register all day."

"Do you have a key to it?"

"Oh, no, Father. He wears the key around his neck."

"What about the toilet?"

"What do you mean, Father?"

"Could anyone have hidden themselves in the toilet during the day?"

She shook her head. "I seldom go there, Father. It isn't fresh and clean like at home."

"Any excitement or arguments among the customers?"

She closed her eyes for a moment. "Don't remember anything, Father."

"Skip to closing time. Were all the customers gone?"

She blushed. "One man remained, wanting me to go to the movie with him. I told him no, so he left. He was the last."

"When did Mr. Ross and the cook leave?"

"Mr. Ross counted the money in the register. Dick turned off the stoves and left before him. Mr. Ross looked about, making sure the café was empty and secure. Then he left, telling me to close up and lock the front door."

"Did you see him lock the register?"

"I was sweeping up by then, but I think I heard him lock it."

"Did you check the back door?"

"No, Father. I did not. There were no deliveries so it hadn't been opened all day.."

"Could it have been unlocked when you were busy with customers?"

She held her hands over her eyes while replying. "Yes, Father. It's possible I suppose. But I didn't notice anyone lounging around the back."

"Go on."

She lowered her hands. "I closed the shades and turned off the lights. Locked the front door as usual and walked home.

"I did not take the money, Father, nor did I help anyone else do it. Please believe me!"

He knelt and gestured. "I believe you.

"Join me, Mary, in a little prayer that soon you will be absolved of this crime."

Prayer over, he made notes on the pad kept from the Connor lunch. "I'm going now to ask Inspector O'Bryan about freeing you. I'll also speak to Mr. Ross about his allegation. Later I'll tell your parents that you're alright and what we're doing.

"Meanwhile, I want you to be as stalwart as Saint Timothy, Mary. We're going to end up as grand as ever."

"Good morning, Inspector."

Without speaking, Inspector O'Bryan handed Murphy the incident report on the Coffee House robbery. "Parishioner of Saint Timothy's or not, here's you another lost cause, Father."

Murphy scanned the paper and looked up. "Fingerprints?"

"The girl's fingerprints were everywhere. So were the prints of Mr. Ross, the owner. The cook's prints were mostly in the kitchen, of course."

"The cash register was broken into? Fingerprints there?"

"You sound like an investigator, Father. Only smudges on the cash register. They probably wore gloves.

"And yes, before you ask. The cash register did have fresh marks on it. It was pried open with some tool."

"They?"

"Crime techs are still working the scene."

Murphy made a few notes. "Have they found anything which could have been used to force open the register?"

At O'Bryan's shake of the head, Murphy added another question. "Any evidence of Mary's guilt in this?"

"You sound like a defense attorney instead of a priest, Father."

Murphy sat down in the chair opposite O'Bryan's desk. "I'm convinced Mary is innocent. I'm just trying to segregate the facts from the chaff."

O'Bryan whistled softly, looking up at his ceiling. "I know you're trying to help, Father, but best leave crime investigations to us, the professionals."

"Be patient with me, Inspector. Did you find the stolen money? How much was it? Was it on Mary?"

"No, Father. She had plenty of time to hide the money after she took it." O'Bryan glanced at a note on his desk. "Mr. Ross reported the missing money totaled Euros 40.98."

"One more question, Inspector. Don't the marks on the register indicate that someone other than Mary took the money?"

"Maybe. But your faith in this girl—to whom you probably taught the catechism— cloud your objectivity, Father. Next you'll be telling me that Mr. Ross stole the money himself!"

Murphy picked up his battered black hat. "Has Ross filed an insurance claim yet? If so, for how much? And does the cook have a bank account? How about checking them out?"

O'Bryan flung up his hands.

FOURTEEN

Mr. James Ross looked up sharply as Father Murphy rapped on the tiny office's door at the Coffee House. Waving Murphy inside, Ross pushed back his chair and put both feet on the desk. "Excuse me, Father, but I might as well get comfortable. I know why you're here. I've already told the police everything I know.

"Which is your sweet, little Mary stole my money and hid it somewhere."

Murphy, uninvited, took a chair facing Ross. "What kind of employee is Mary, Mr. Ross?"

He lit a cigarette. "No complaints."

"She's been with you long?"

"Coupla' of years, Father."

"Hear many complaints about her from your customers?"

"Our customers are mostly men. None of them complain, except that she won't give them the time of day. Smart girl," Ross added, tipping ash into a saucer.

"If she acted like some other waitresses, I'd have fired her long ago."

"Sounds like an exemplary employee, Mr. Ross."

Ross stretched. "Say what you want, Father. The money's gone. Either she took it herself or helped someone steal it."

"Why would she risk a good job for only a payback of 40-odd euros?"

Ross shrugged. "Maybe she wanted to get her hair done. Who knows?"

"Were your missing money refunded, would you drop charges against Mary?"

Ross removed his feet from the desk. "You mean 'returned,' not refunded, don't you?"

"Either way," Murphy persisted. "And would you also agree to keep her employed?"

He lit another cigarette. "Is that your deal, Father?"

"It is, because I'm convinced that sweet little Mary—as you call her—is innocent. If I can, I'm going to help the police find the real thief.

"Your customers wouldn't think kindly if Mary were treated unfairly by your establishment. Would they?

"Please call me at Saint Timothy's tomorrow with your decision, Mr. Ross."

Once back at his desk, Murphy telephoned the Canadys to tell them how Mary was faring in jail and what he was attempting to do.

"Does that mean you think our daughter's innocent, Father?"

"I think that's a strong possibility, Mrs. Canady, which I'm attempting to prove, with the help of the police, of course."

Viola stood at the door, overhearing the conversation. "You're a great, good man, Father!"

Tears glistened in her eyes as she patted his shoulder. "A perfect man!" she whispered wistfully.

Ten minutes later she was answering the church's telephone. "Hello?"

"Did you get one, too, Viola?"

"Get what, Joyce?"

"An engraved invitation to have tea with Maude Connor? Mine just came in the mail. I bet you're invited, too."

"No. Mail hasn't come here yet. When's the big event?"

"Tomorrow morning at eleven. I'm off to town now to have my hair and nails done. You know how Maude dresses up, even for vestry meetings."

"What's it about?"

"Dunno. Must be something about the church."

"She's after something and I can guess what it is."

"Tell me."

"Not over the phone. I'll call you if I get an invitation. We can go together."

"Suppose Maude will be wearing her tiara?"

The pair knocked on the Connor door at the appointed time, immediately greeted by Eunice, the housekeeper.

Maude Connor stood in the parlor, glancing at her gold watch. Beside her was a cowed young girl. "You ladies are very prompt."

"Rose. This is Mrs. MacDoo and Miss Norton. My niece, Rose, ladies. Rose is daughter of my sister Cornelia in Dunsmore.

"Shall we all have a chair? I've asked Rose here to entertain us with her recitation of the famous Irish poem for which she just won a school prize."

Smiling uncertainly, Viola and Joyce nodded and sat down.

"I've promised Rose an extra treat in the kitchen if she remembers all the words of the poem."

Still standing, Rose took a deep breath and began slowly reciting:

I will rise and go now, and go to Innisfree,

> *And a small cabin build there of clay and*
> *wattles made,*
> *Nine bean rows will I have there, a hive for*
> *honey bees*

Nora looked at Viola and winked. Like a metronome, Maude Connor was keeping time with a raised finger

> *And live alone in the bee loud glade,*
> concentrating, Rose breathed heavily.
> *I will arise and go now, for...*she blushed at
> the forgotten words,
> *I hear lake waters lapping with low sounds*
> *by the shore!*

She finished with a little bow to their applause.

"That was splendid, Rose," Viola began. Joyce echoed with "Well done!"

Connor was less effusive, frowning at the missed words. "Thank you, Rose. You may go to the kitchen now and ask for your treat. Please tell the cook to serve us tea."

Immediately, Annie, the cook, emerged from the kitchen carrying a large, heavily loaded silver tray. She set it on the table with an effort.

With a nod, Annie left and Connor took charge of serving her wary guests.

"Thank you," Joyce acknowledged, accepting a cup, saucer and napkin.

"I hope you enjoy the tea. It's Earl Grey, my favorite."

"Thank you, Maude," Viola said. "Your invitation was a nice surprise."

The three sat, sipping tea, studying each other.

Connor broke the silence. "Thanks to you both for coming on such short notice. I thought we should exchange ideas on future vestry activities for the good of our congregation as well as the town. Father Murphy would make the final decision on whatever action the vestry suggests, but I thought it useful for us to discuss a particular favorite of mine."

Connor paused to sip her tea, willing Joyce to voice the question. Watchful, Viola sat back sipping tea, knowing what Connor had proposed during her luncheon with Father Murphy.

Joyce stammered, "Wha…what is your favorite idea, Maude?"

Smiling at Joyce's expression, Connor refilled her cup. "I suggest that the public parks in town be closed during the hours of darkness. I understand they are bee-hives of activity after hours, most of it illicit, illegal or immoral."

Shaking her head dramatically, Connor pursed her lips. "What are your thoughts, ladies?"

Joyce swallowed a mouthful of tea, almost coughing. "Well, I guess your suggestion might be a good one. Maybe there'd be less crime in the 'bee-hives' as you call them, were closed at night."

Viola countered. "I know many of our parish families lack greens or gardens to enjoy after work. Have you asked the police for their record of illegal activities in the parks at night?"

Connor frowned. "Naturally, I'm asking the police to gather such information. We can present their findings, statistics—or whatever—at the next vestry meeting. When is that scheduled Viola?"

"There's nothing on the Father's calendar for vestry meetings at the moment, Maude. He's been quite active lately with the youth group, the tractor pull, preparing for the Bishop's visit and other things."

Joyce brightened. "Perhaps it would be better if we had the statistics in hand and studied them before calling for a meeting."

Connor, looking sullen, referred to notes at her elbow. "There are a few other ideas on which I'd like your opinions, since we're deferring the park suggestion.

"Next, the public swimming pool," she rang the bell for a hot pot of tea. "Don't you think pool usage should be segregated? Ladies in the morning and gentlemen in the afternoon?

"And on that same subject, I definitely think there should be restrictions on the type of bathing attire worn in the pool, particularly by females."

Connor challenged Viola. "Your thoughts, dear?"

Viola smiled. "Like you, I find bikinis and cut-offs worn in the pool unseemly. But if the pools were segregated by sex, many folks would miss family outings and swimming parties."

She turned, seeking reinforcement. "What do you think, Joyce?"

"Well, I'd want to accompany my husband, Ron, when he goes swimming. I suppose most wives feel the same."

Answering the bell, the housekeeper appeared at the door.

"Please clear the table, Eunice," Connor began, crumpling her notes in one hand.

"Thank you for coming ladies and your frank views.

Perhaps we can meet again when I have more data from the police on what goes on in the parks at night."

Connor stood, forcing her guests do the same. "Eunice will see you to the door, ladies. Thank you again and good afternoon."

On the sidewalk outside, Joyce punched Viola playfully. "You really upset 'Her Ladyship', didn't you?"

"Didn't we?" Viola punched her back. "Notice that big tray of biscuits on the sideboard? Strange we weren't offered some with our tea."

"They might have been poisoned," Joyce laughed.

Upstairs, behind a curtain, an angry Connor watched their hilarity.

FIFTEEN

Honk, honk! "Hey Cherie! It's me!" The van sled to a stop beside the girl in the crosswalk.

She stopped midway across the road, staring.

"Joe, you got us a car!" she trilled.

"Get in," he yelled, opening the passenger door. "I'll tell you all about it."

She slid across the seat toward him. "Nice big car or whatever it's called. How'd you get it?"

Immediately, she scooted back to the passenger door and attempted to open it. "Stole it, did you? Let me out!" she screamed.

"No, no! Calm down, Cherie! I didn't steal it. I got a job!"

Mollified, she lit a cigarette, opened a window and stared at him. "Tell the truth, Joe. You got a job? Who'd hire an ex-con?"

She scooted back beside him and gripped his knee. "The truth, for a change!"

"Honest, sweet. I read the jobs column in the *Journal*, emailed a site and got hired the same day!"

She lit another cigarette and passed it to him. "Doin' what?"

"Driving and maintaining this almost-new Nissan SUV for a Mr. Evers in Kinsale. He liked me right away when I said I'm from Mallow. If I do well, he'll have some special work for me over here. With premium pay!"

She curled her arm about his neck. "Doin' what?" she repeated. "And what's the pay?"

"Get my first check the end of the week. I start at 100 euros a week. All I do is phone him, he tells me where to take people for their meetings. I wait and bring them back to Kinsale or wherever. Great job, huh? Even my mom would be pleased.

"Now you can move back in with me." He kissed her ear. "I'm a gombeen, I miss you so much."

She didn't avoid this kiss. "I'll think it awhile. By the way, where is your mom? You never talk about her. Why is that?"

"She's angry with me that I've been in prison. Not my fault I was caught. That old woman with the airs reported me to the police."

"Who?"

"That Connor woman, the one they call 'Her Ladyship.'"

Cherie voiced another, more persistent thought. "Got any money on you?"

"Just a few coins. But I'll get paid soon."

"Still got that pistol?"

"Sure."

"Why not sell it to tide us over a few days? It's bound to worth a lot more than a thousand. What do you say, lover?"

After evening prayers, Murphy sat down in his office, conceding he felt tired. Scheduled that night to attend a youth group meeting planning its annual carnival, he instead considered going directly to bed. Let Viola take the meeting for him. Sleep, redeeming sleep, was what he needed most.

Shaking his head, he said aloud, "I must be getting old," to his reflection in the office window.

Viola stood in the open door, studying him. "You're not at all old, Father. I'd say you are in splendid shape. May I come in?"

"Of course," he grinned, wondering how long she'd been standing there. He was tempted to repeat the 'splendid shape' comment about her, but refrained.

"Mary Canady is here, wanting to see you, Father. I think she intends to thank you for your efforts on her behalf."

Murphy stood, to clear his mind of both rest and thoughts of his administrator's shape. "Hurray! A small victory!"

Mary matched his mood. "Oh, Father," she gushed. "I can't possibly thank you for all that you did for me. Mr. Ross withdrew his charges against me, so the police let me go. He even let me keep my job! Thank you!"

"Did he say anything else?"

"Only that I was a good employee. He did make a change in our closing routine. Now the last one out—whether him or me—completes a little checklist. Like making sure the toilets not running, the backdoor bolted, stoves and ovens off, lights out and front door locked. One of us initials the checklist, marks the time and leaves it by the cash register.

"Oh! My parents thank you, too, Father. They are so relieved that I'm home and won't be charged."

"Have you a moment, Mary? I've thought of some questions about what you told me the other day.

She nodded.

"Have a seat, please," he said.

Viola still stood at the door. "Would you like tea, Father?"

"Grand idea! We'll celebrate. Tea for you, too."

Once Mrs. Casey delivered the tea tray, Viola insisted on pouring three cups and handing them out.

"Now, Mary. I keep thinking about that last customer in your shop the night of the robbery. Remember what you said?"

"Yes, Father."

"Did you know the last customer?"

"Not by name, Father. He's often there for coffee, usually sits by himself as if he isn't real chummy with the others."

"You remember he was the last to leave because he asked you out?"

"Yes, Father. That was a bit odd. He asked if I had a car there. If I did, he invited to take me to the movie house in Kanturk. His car was in shop and he wanted to see 'Beauty and the Beast' over there."

"I told him no, thanks. I didn't have a car there and I never go out with customers. That's one of Mr. Ross's rules."

"So the man left and you closed the shop?"

"Yes, Father. Why?"

Murphy blew on his hot tea. "I was wondering if that man, or any of the others, could have slipped by you and unbolted the back door while you were busy serving?"

Mary hesitated. "I suppose it's possible, but Mr. Ross was there, too. He would have noticed something like that."

Viola and Mary looked at each other. Mary fidgeted with another thought. "Uh, Father?"

"Yes?" Murphy checked his watch. The youth group met in fifteen minutes.

"I just remembered that Mr. Ross went to the back, probably to the toilet for a minute. I guess someone could have unbolted the door while he was in there."

"Perhaps so, perhaps so," Murphy frowned, tea forgotten.

"Do you remember how the man who asked you to the movie was dressed?"

"Just like the rest. Well...except he had a small tool sack

and work gloves. Said he had no place to leave them until he went home because his car was being repaired."

"Thank you, Mary. If you can remember his name or the name of the repair shop, please call me.

"Thanks to you, too, Viola, for the tea. It revived my doldrums. Please thank Mrs. Casey for us."

Murphy stood, rubbing his jaw in thought.

Seeing his absent look, Viola whispered a reminder as she and Mary left. "The youth group meeting, Father."

SIXTEEN

"The meeting will come to order," Joyce intoned officially while opening her notebook "Father, Mrs. Kennedy has asked to begin tonight's discussion."

"Thank you, Joyce." Kennedy smiled at Murphy.

"Father, this is a special meeting of the vestry to present you a problem as well as a possible solution. The problem is the organization of a large, representative committee of citizens for the purpose of planning and overseeing the 500th anniversary celebration of Mallow Castle. It will be an event publicized throughout Ireland. The success—or lack thereof—will reflect on our city and our county as well as Saint Timothy's."

Murphy nodded appreciatively, causing the vestry members to nod encouragement at their spokeswoman.

"We think, Father, that Saint Timothy's should be represented on this anniversary by the best qualified candidate we can offer. We have an outstanding, well-known and respected candidate right here on our vestry, Maude Connor."

Turning from Murphy, Kennedy winked at the other members before continuing. "Were she present here tonight, extreme modesty would preclude her accepting this candidacy despite her high qualifications for this prestigious position."

Murphy raised a hand. "What position?"

Kennedy appeared surprised at the question. "Maude Connor should not only represent Saint Timothy's on this planning committee, Father, she's so talented, she should be its chairperson!"

She looked at the others for confirmation. 'Ayes!' resounded from each member.

Father Murphy looked about the table, suspecting complicity. "How do you expect Maude to react to your idea?"

Kennedy smiled. "We think she will be thrilled if you personally voiced our unanimous support of her candidacy for this position. Saint Timothy's and Mallow both will be well represented by Maude Connor.

"Unfortunately," Kennedy turned solemn, "the press of the heavy responsibilities to guide the 500th anniversary's planning and execution would preclude her active participation in our vestry for some time."

Suspicious, Murphy turned to the others, receiving sage nods from all.

"Very well, since you seem in agreement, we'll discuss this matter at our next regular," he emphasized, "regular vestry meeting scheduled for…?"

He looked at Viola.

"Next Tuesday after evening prayers, with your approval, Father."

He looked thoughtful, but nodded.

"Meeting adjourned," announced Joyce.

As the others filed out, Murphy touched her arm. "I'd like to see you in my office, Viola."

"We've found us a pot o' gold, Cherie!"

He uncovered her face, covered by dingy bedclothes. "Did ya' hear me? A pot of gold!"

She coughed and spit into a tissue. "Quit ya' screeching, gombeen! Where's the gold? Show me."

He shoved her over on the mattress. "It's as good as in the Bank of Ireland. Just listen, love. My boss, Mr. Evers, strange feen that he is, wants me to draw him an interior map of Saint Timothy's. He wants it to show all the rooms, galleries, closets, niches, altar...everything!"

"Don't do it, Joe. He sounds like a terrorist or somethin'. Maybe he plans to bomb the place. Why else would he need a map of a church?"

"No, no. None of that. He wants to build a new temple for what he calls his congregation in Kinsale. He likes Saint Timothy's layout so well, he wants his new place to be a mirror image of it."

"What's he paying?"

"Three hundred if my map's really accurate, he says. Three hundred'll get us a better place, some new clothes for you, maybe even a trip to the Ring of Kerry!"

Cherie sat up, clutching a pillow. "We are overdue for a new place to hide but are you sure this is all legal, Joe?"

"What else could it be, doll?"

"Why doesn't this guy just go and buy a map, or something?"

"It's got to be architecturally correct in every detail to be able to reproduce it in his own place. One other thing... very important," he drew her closer.

She yelped. "You're scratching me!"

She pushed him away, curiosity overcoming irritation. "What is it?"

"I can't tell anybody, including you, about this job. I can't even tell my own mother. Strictly confidential! Got it? No talking to anyone about the job or the money we're going to make."

She brightened. "Maybe he'd like to buy that pistol, too."

Viola followed Murphy into the office. She caught her breath as he shut the door behind her.

Trying to appear normal, she asked. "You wanted to see me, Father?"

He motioned her to the chair in front of his desk. He packed a pipe while studying her. "Mind if I smoke?"

She held her breath at the ease of his first question. "Of course not, Father."

"Have you anything to tell me about Mrs. Kennedy's proposal? I'm guessing you knew about it long before today."

Blushing, she stared at her hands in her lap. "Yes, Father, I knew what she was going to say. We all did."

"Why didn't you forewarn me, Viola? You're my strong right arm, like Timothy and Paul."

Almost in tears, she looked up. He handed her the box of tissues from the desk.

"Forgive me, Father. In my defense, I thought you felt about Maude just like we all do. I should have prepared you for that meeting.

"She would be a grand chairperson for that anniversary committee," she added defensively.

"You have a point there. Meanwhile let's try to be more communicative with each other. I'm sure I've been equally guilty, haven't I?"

"Well…," she hesitated. "Sometimes, Father, you forget to tell me things, like why you went to the police. Perhaps I could be more helpful if I knew the reasons."

He reached out a hand as he stood. "I apologize and

will try to be more forthcoming. Like now, I should call Inspector O'Bryan and tell him what I suspect about the robbery of the Coffee House and who the culprit may be."

He paused, reaching for the telephone. "Did Mary call with any information about the man who asked her to the movies?"

"No, Father."

"Or what auto shop has his car?"

She shook her head, anxious to tell him something else before he disappeared. "It's me who should apologize, Father, not you. I intend to be the best administrator for you I possibly can."

After Viola left, he picked up the telephone and dialed police headquarters and asked for an appointment with Inspector O'Bryan.

SEVENTEEN

Twenty minutes after Murphy pedaled off to the police station, the church telephone rang again. Viola answered.

"Good day, is this Saint Timothy's?"

"Yes, it is. Miss Norton speaking. How may I be of assistance?"

There was a pause. "Well, Viola, I'm surprised you do not recognize my voice. This is Mrs. Connor. I urgently need to speak to the Father."

"Sorry, Mrs. Connor," Viola returned the formality. "Father Murphy is not here at the moment. He's what he calls 'liasing' with the police."

Connor became more strident. "I repeat, I must speak to him immediately. Contact him and ask him to return to the rectory immediately."

"I'll do that, Mrs. Connor, but if there is an emergency perhaps I can help."

"Father must be here in twenty minutes, that's the emergency. I'm donating a large sum of money to the church's Youth Council and the ceremony is to be in front of Saint Timothy's within twenty…no…eighteen minutes.

"Press coverage, both a reporter and a photographer have been arranged to be here in a few minutes. I'm standing here on the church steps, waiting.

"I must say, Miss Norton, you're being most unhelpful. Father must return here immediately!"

Frowning, Viola checked her copy of Murphy's schedule. "Does the Father already know of this event? It's not on his calendar."

"Really, Miss Norton, if it were on the calendar, he'd be at Saint Timothy's already. Perhaps he forgot to post it."

Viola wished she'd had a second cup of strong tea. "I maintain the Father's calendar for him, Mrs. Connor. I'm certain that the Father is unaware of this event. Unless you told him. Did you?"

Connor's voice rose an octave "That's beside the point! He's supposed to be readily available at all hours to his parishioners. My ancestors have been here since the Normans. We...we established Saint Timothy's!"

She paused to catch her breath, resumed ranting even louder. "Being among the oldest members of this parish, I expect him to give the utmost service, especially since I personally am making a large donation to one of his favorite groups, our youth."

"I'm calling the police station, Maude," she emphasized the first name. Viola punched her cell phone and had a minute-long conversation with someone at the station.

She held the cell phone to one ear while relaying the information to Connor from the landline in the other ear. "Father Murphy left the station about ten minutes ago and is believed to be returning to Saint Timothy's on his bicycle.

"I suggest you hold the reporter and photographer in front until he returns. I'd further suggest that you discuss with me in advance anything you desire to add to his busy schedule."

Connor's reply was to smash her telephone in the receiver.

Cub reporter Dennis Hyde rushed his latest article of the week to his boss, the editor of the Mallow *Journal* that morning. Deadline for the *Journal's* morning edition was noon, unless there was a national holiday.

He thrust his single-page copy at editor Bruton, who stared at the copy. "You must have made it to Saint Timothy's in time."

Hyde smiled. His editor was a hardnosed newspaperman who gave few accolades, especially to cub reporters.

As Bruton read the copy, Hyde watched a pair of flies crawling on Bruton's old-fashioned metal lunch box. His stood straighter as—of all things—Bruton began reading Hyde's article aloud.

YOUTH GROUP GAINS A BONANZA

The daughter of Mallow's founding family, Mrs. Maude Connor, donated E1,000. to the Youth Group of Saint Timothy's Church today.

Connor of Northside's Manor House said the gift is to "encourage and grow" more healthy activities for today's young people, not only at Saint Timothy's but throughout our city and county.

"A current project of the Youth Group," according to Connor, "is a fall themed carnival of athletic games, baking contests, silent auctions, a fashion show and music provided by five local youth bands.

"As a senior member of Saint Timothy's, I encourage all ages to attend this family-friendly carnival which will provide funding for future Youth Group fetes."

Receiving the generous donation was Father A.T. Murphy, rector of Saint Timothy's.

CAPTION: Holding aloft her donation cheque for Saint Timothy's Youth Group is Mrs. Maude Connor. In the background is Saint Timothy's Church.

Bruton looked from the copy to Hyde and sneered. "This rich old lady must have bought your lunch, eh? This article is too short. You spent too many words on this Connor person instead of the kids."

"I should make you rewrite the whole thing but it's press time," he checked his watch, "and the paper's almost in bed."

He shook his finger at the crestfallen reporter. "You should have concentrated on the Youth Group, not the old lady. And where are the photos? We're holding a spot for at least one photo on the front page."

"Here they are, sir," Hyde held out the two photographs.

Bruton examined them closely. "Both are of the old woman standing in front of the church, holding up her donation. No member of the Youth Group or maybe its president? None of the priest, either?"

"Sir, she insisted on these photos: only her and the cheque."

"Remember you're the reporter, the professional journalist, not her."

"I'll only use one photo. Now get out of here. And write better copy next time!"

Mrs. Casey greeted Father Murphy with a tray of two hot teas as he entered the office. "Here, Father, you'll be needing this."

"What's wrong?"

Casey nodded toward Viola's door. "She's in there

92

crying, Father. It's about that terrible Maude Connor and what she said to Viola before you returned from the police."

"What did she say?"

"Best to come from Viola, Father. She's in need of a little pastoral attention at the moment, if you'll excuse my impertinence."

He walked to the closed door and heard crying inside. Knocking gently, he said, "May I come in, Viola?"

Wiping reddened eyes, Viola opened the door. "Yes, Father?" she sniffled. "What may I do for you?"

He placed the tea tray on her desk. "Let's start with a cup of Mrs. Casey's freshly-brewed tea. Okay?

"Remember, you and I were going to communicate better with each other."

Viola looked away and wiped her eyes again. "Yes, Father. I'm ashamed that you see me here like this."

"Tell me what Maude said."

She hesitated, taking a new tissue. "I don't want to be the cause of bad feelings between you and Maude, Father."

"I know. Tell me what she said that upset you."

"Father, did you know she was coming here with a reporter and photographer from the *Journal?*"

"No, I didn't. I pedaled here from the police station and she and the two young men were waiting for me in front of the church. She told me that she wanted to present me a cheque for the Youth Organization's carnival.

"I said certainly, thank you. The photographer snapped pictures of her and the three of them left. She must have said something scathing to you. What was it?"

Viola nodded, compressing her lips. "She said I was most unhelpful when I told her you were not here and where you'd gone. She became very upset with me. It was the way she said it. She made me feel like I'm a terrible person and an even worse administrator.

"I'm truly sorry I told you, Father. I must be tougher. Forgive me, please."

He patted her hand. "Let's drink the tea before it gets cold," he raised his cup. "My hope is that *you* forgive her."

EIGHTEEN

Ruth held out the morning's edition of the *Journal* to Mrs. Kennedy, sitting at the dining table. "Scandalous, I calls it. Wait 'til you read what that woman's done today!"

"Who? What woman?"

Ruth sniffed. "That Maude Connor is who. Look here."

Kennedy adjusted her glasses to scan the front page. "Where, Ruth? Oh, I see it."

She read the article twice than glanced at the captioned photo. Handing the paper back to Ruth, she sighed. "All that publicity for a tax-deductible E1,000! Smart old schemer, I'd say!"

Under her breath she added, "Somebody's got to stop that woman. Perhaps it should be…"

Rather than risk driving the SUV, its Temple of the Augury markings easily recognized or remembered, Cheri and Joe walked the two miles to Saint Timothy's.

"I'm daft to come here with you," she muttered.

"Quiet, quiet," he placed his hand over her mouth.

She bit him.

"Ay," he muffled a curse, holding the hand.

"Quiet, quiet," she mocked him.

Stealthily they entered the church through a small door leading to the sacristy. Once inside, she nudged him. "How'd ya' know that one was unlocked?"

"I asked around," he whispered. "Did my homework, I did. Even got an interior sketch of the place from the Survey Office in Cork."

"Then why do we have to be here in the dark, measuring it if you already have a sketch or something?"

He turned to her and snapped off the flashlight. "Because what we're doing here is a secret. Nobody is to know why we are here. Mr. Evers doesn't want it known that Saint Timothy's is going to be duplicated in his new temple at Kinsale."

"How much did you say we get?"

He was pacing the back and sides of the robing area of the narrow room and counting steps. "Write down three meters by three by two for the sacristy."

Irritated, she raised her voice. "That doesn't make sense!"

"Just write it down," he hissed. "I'll explain later."

"You didn't answer my question."

He was pacing the sacristy corridor. "Quit distracting me. Write down three by six. What question?"

"How much do we get?"

"Three hundred if it's accurate enough for an architectural plan. Now, help me quietly, instead of niggling."

Opening the door to the interior of the church, he began pacing from the sacristy door to the middle of the tabernacle. Then he paced to the opposite wall. Happy with the measurements, he whispered the numbers to her and she noted them on a pad.

Next he paced from the tabernacle to the altar, from the altar to the lectern and to the baptismal font. Repeating numbers to her, he stepped down to the pew area of the nave, pacing it from front to rear and from side to side.

They climbed the short stairs to the organ where he repeated measuring the area and whispering dimensions to her.

"Do we really have to whisper?" she demanded.

"I've been here at night several times watching the church, readying for this job. I've seen *Garda* patrol cars drive by, even policemen getting out to check doors and lights."

He stopped and consulted a luminous watch. "It'll be daylight in an hour. We've got to get out now the same way we got in."

"Aren't we through? It's cold in here."

"No, we'll have to come again. Can't stay too long or we'd be noticed.

"If we are seen or heard here, the whole deal's off and we get no money. I told you that, remember?"

She turned off her small penlight. "This place gives me the jeebies. It's like a tomb. Let's get the hell out of here."

Once outside, they quickly walked back to the still-darkened area where they left the Tucson. Once inside the SUV, he stretched and grinned.

"That was a cake-walk, wasn't it? We'll be back tonight to finish the job."

John Long's bar was filled with noisy men except in the back corner, where it was quiet. John Reilly, George Bailey and Pat Davis sat enjoying their pints and intermittently staring at one another or the football game on the television.

Pat broke the silence. "The way I'm thinking, we need another plan."

"For what?" George asked.

"This thing about ousting old Maude will come to a head at the next vestry meet. We need a plan to make sure she accepts our sending her off to that celebration committee."

"And out of our hair," John added. "Our thinning hair," he smirked, patting his own. "What can we do?"

"Somehow we need to embarrass her so she accepts being exiled to that committee. Any ideas?"

George voiced one. "Sure! How about another round?" He gestured to Sean, the barman.

"Let's get a photo of old Maude givin' her gardener a shift. Then get the papers to publish it."

"Or just circulate it among the town council."

"No, we'd have to pay the gardener more money than the three of us have," George joked.

Pat scratched his beard. "Embarrass, embarrass... How do we embarrass 'Her Ladyship'? Ought to be easy."

George turned to John. "What do you use when your cows are birthin' to calm them down?"

"If they're uneasy or in pain, I give them a shot of something called Rompon. That settles them every time."

"Can it be used on humans?"

"No. We don't want to kill her, just sedate her a bit."

"Rompon has to be injected," John shook his head.

"Out of the question," George accepted a new pint from the barman. "Sean, can we borrow a paper and pen from you for a minute?"

Sean handed George the paper and pen.

George passed it to Pat. "Here, Pat. You're our best writer."

"What's this for?"

"You mentioned the newspaper, Pat. How about an advertisement in the paper from Maude, seeking the company of a man? Wouldn't that do the trick? Everybody would see it in the personals column and make fun of her."

John was enthusiastic. "Great idea. Write us an ad,

Pat. She'd be so embarrassed, she won't even come to vestry meetings."

Pat frowned at the paper before him, began alternately writing, then crossing out words. John and George were silent until the writing was over.

"Read it, Pat."

He took a drink, cleared his throat and began.

PERSONAL: "Elegant, cultured Mallow lady seeks a mature, educated gentleman for companionship and conversation. Reply with précis and photo to Box 1234, the Cork Independent, Attn: M.C."

Pat waved his paper overhead. "How's that, chums?"

"Massive!" George was first.

"Fantastic!" John agreed.

"We'll send it with a ten spot to the newspaper in Cork, without a return address or name."

George raised his pint to Pat. "Well done!"

Grinning, John wiped spilled drink from his beard. "Placing just her initials at the end is absolutely brilliant, Pat! Everyone in Mallow will immediately know who placed the ad."

Pat clasped his hands above him like a prizefighter. "There's one more thing if this advertisement doesn't do the trick."

"Wha's that?"

"Ask Viola to have tea served at the vestry meeting. Maude's tea gets a double dram of Jameson's in it when she's not looking."

In unison, the three shouted, "Another round, Sean!"

Loudly, even before the pints arrived, they began loudly singing:

> *There was a wild colonial boy*
> *Jack Duggan was his name.*
> *He was born and bred in Ireland....*

NINETEEN

Viola's desk telephone clamored that afternoon. She swiveled her chair about to answer.

"Inspector O'Bryan here, may I speak to the Father, please?"

"Sorry, Inspector," she double-checked his schedule, already knowing where he was at that hour. "Father Murphy's conducting Stations of the Cross to a large crowd, followed by evening vespers. He won't be available until later. May I give him a message?"

O'Bryan hesitated, searching for the report he wanted to share. "Oh, well," he was about to give up but found it on the bottom of a stack.

"Please tell the Father that we have a lead on the man he called me about involved in that Coffee House burglary."

"Yes, Inspector?"

"I think we may have identified that man and are searching for both him and the female fugitive. We think they may be together again."

"I relay that to the Father. Anything more, sir?"

"No, thank you."

That night on Balsam Street, across from Saint Timothy's, Cherie and Joe sat on a bench, watching people file out the church and shake hands with a priest.

She pointed. "That's the one who helped the police."

"Aye, I see the gobshite. He's going to pay dearly for

that. Meanwhile. he and Saint Timothy's are providing us E300. worth of easy work."

She resisted the urge to light a cigarette "I hope we finish the job tonight. I don't like bein' in that creepy place."

"After they're all out, we'll wait an hour then go in and finish up."

It was nearly midnight when they entered the church by the same small unlocked door they'd used before. "Quiet, now," he hissed, listening for any noise.

Satisfied after a wait, they began measuring the adjacent parlor and waiting rooms. He paced each area and she recorded the numbers.

By the front door, they repeated the process in the vestibule and cloak rooms. Turning about, they studied the vastness of the nave.

"What's that there?"

"Where do you mean?" he asked, not wanting to shine the flashlight unnecessarily.

"Looks like a closet—or something—next to what you called the tabernacle."

"There's a little serving table inside the closet. There's a white cloth on it, maybe for tea?"

She punched his shoulder. "Don't be silly. They don't serve tea in here."

They walked up the main aisle, past the rails and stood before the enclosure. She opened a cabinet door and caught her breath.

"Look at all that shiny silver, Joe! Big cups, saucers, too! It all looks like the real stuff."

She held up a big silver chalice and a paten. "Heavy!

And there are several more in here. What'll you think we could get for these?"

He hefted the chalice. "Solid silver, I bet. Must be worth a lot. Silver is easy to sell anywhere!"

Someone rattled the church front door.

"Shh! Hear that, Joe?"

His voice shook. "Let's get out of here."

She held another big chalice in her hand and gestured to the other one. "What about these?"

"Bring them," he whispered. "Move it! Fast and quiet!"

Viola and Murphy had just finished breakfast and he was somewhere in the church when Maude Connor barged into Viola's office.

"Where is he?" she demanded, eyes blazing. "I want to see him right this minute!"

Accustomed to protecting Murphy from wild-eyed people in the early morning, Viola held up a restraining hand. "Perhaps I can be of assistance, Maude."

"Where is he?" Anger colored Connor's protruding cheeks. Out of breath, she stuttered. "Ware iss he?"

"Please have a seat and I'll fetch the Father for you. Perhaps a cup of tea while you wait?"

'And calm down?' Viola thought to herself.

The word 'wait' cleared Connor's stutter. "I'll look for him myself! Which way did he go?"

"Please sit down, Mrs. Connor," Viola tried again. "I'll locate the Father and tell him you are here."

"You're absolutely no use," Connor pushed Viola back into her chair. "I'll find him myself!"

The open door to the nave provided a clue and Connor

leaped through it, into a side aisle. Viola followed close behind, wishing she'd accepted Father Murphy's offer of a pepper spray for protection.

"There he is!" Connor bellowed, seeing Murphy praying at the altar rail.

Viola tried to grab an arm to restrain Connor. "Control yourself, Maude, this is a church. He's praying. Don't be acting the maggot!"

Connor shook off Viola and stood beside Father Murphy, his eyes closed, his lips silently moving.

Startled, he looked up.

"Stand up, Father!" Connor's command resounded in the near-empty church. "Have you read this?" She thrust a newspaper into Murphy's hands.

He stood, frowning at the newsprint. "We don't take this paper. Can't afford it."

She grabbed the newspaper from his hands and turned to the classified section.

"Read this, Father! I'm being treated terribly by some vicious person, probably from this very church!"

Murphy sat down in the front pew to read the advertisement she pointed at with trembling hand.

"Someone is smearing my good name in Mallow and I want you to take action about it at the very next service."

Murphy scanned the ad again and passed it to Viola, now seated beside him. "I take it you did not place this notice in the newspaper?"

She shrieked. "Of course not! What a question! If I knew who placed this ad I'd have them arrested and locked up, awaiting trial!

"Father, my family founded this town and this church.

I expect you immediately to denounce this as a false, vicious attempt to make me the laughing stock of Mallow."

Viola interrupted. "Maude, if the Father did that, everyone immediately would know about the ad, then perhaps ridicule you. Not everyone here takes the paper. I suggest that keeping quiet about this injustice is the better response, rather than going public with it."

"Good point, Viola," Murphy said. "Don't you agree, Maude?"

So enraged her eyes looked like black pin points, Connor shook her fist at them.

Taking a deep breath, she bolted for the front door, yelling over her shoulder. "If you don't do as I ask, I'll tell the Monsignor—an old family friend—to transfer both of you to the Aran Islands!"

Father Murphy took the threat calmly, not even forgetting his usual "Bless you, Maude."

Smiling to herself, Viola was thinking. 'At least we'd still be together.'

TWENTY

"Great news, Father!" It was Inspector O'Bryan on the telephone again, in an uncharacteristic mood. "We've found the Sig Sauer pistol taken from the police guard by that young woman who escaped from our van. It had been pawned in a shop in Kinsale."

"Can you identify the person who sold it?"

"That's the rub, Father. That shop owner claims his firearms records were destroyed by fire last week."

"How convenient."

"I know, I know. But we've got several leads on the man who sold it, including a good description."

"Speaking of convenience, may I tell you about a robbery in Saint Timothy's that happened today?"

"You mean the missing silver items? I read the telephone report we received. What else can you tell me?"

"Two antique silver paten and two silver chalices are missing. They are highly valuable both from their sacramental and monetary aspects. They were discovered missing this morning by my administrator, Viola Norton, whom you know. I regret they were in an unlocked cabinet next to the tabernacle.

"I also regret we didn't have the necessary funds to insure them." He shrugged. "You see, we recently increased our pledge of support for missions in Nigeria.

"Saint Timothy's will be forever grateful to you and the *Garda* if they can be returned. I'm already instituting more security measures, to include a hidden camera in the chapel. No one, not even Viola or Amos knows where it is."

"Good, good," O'Bryan said. "I'll try to increase patrolling around your church, Father."

"We will remember you and the *Garda* in our prayers for your safety, Inspector."

She slapped the hand offering her the money. "That's all you got for the pistol...*my* pistol?"

At his startled nod, she punched him. "It was worth ten times that!" She threw the money on the floor of their just-rented cottage.

"Why is it that everything you touch goes arseways?

"Besides that," she caught her breath, "don't you know the police are lookin' right now for the dumb muppet who publicly sold a police pistol?"

Joe touched his cheek with a hand to see if there was blood. "I told the guy that I'd found it in a ditch outside a' town. He believed me, even said I was a good citizen for bringing it in.

"Besides, we just got here," he gestured about, "I ain't going nowhere."

Studying him, Cherie sat down and lit a new cigarette from the previous. "We still got that E300. comin' from that Temple bunch?"

"Of course."

"Let's go get it now. We'll need it to pay the rent on this place since you seem to love it here.

"That silver junk still in the boot of the SUV?"

"Where else?" He felt of his cheek again. "You'd better not think you'll get away with hitting me again, love."

"Love!" she snorted. "That's a laugh. Now, give me the keys and we're off to Kinsale for that money."

She paused at the door. "Hi! You don't think that Evers guy'll want the SUV back, do you?"

"No reason." Joe proudly hooked thumbs in his jacket. "I'm still on the payroll for hauling his followers around from place to place. Now do you love me?"

Viola and Mrs. Casey were at a kitchen table dicing vegetables for the evening's soup when Viola's cell phone sounded a tune. "Aye?" she answered.

"Mrs. Kennedy here, Viola. Isn't it time we scheduled that vestry meeting to rid ourselves of Maude Connor?"

"Yes, Mrs. Kennedy. I'll ask the Father if Wednesday evening's alright. Do you think we're fully prepared?"

Kennedy chuckled. "With that recent 'personal heart-seeking man' ad in the classifieds, I don't see how we can miss. Maude must be devastated. She may be too ashamed to even attend her last vestry meeting."

"Oh, no! She's feisty as ever. Even wants the Father—how did she put it—to denounce the advertisement as false and slanderous from the lectern. 'The person who placed it should be arrested and put away,' she said. She even threatened Father if he failed to announce what she wanted…"

"What was her threat?"

"If he doesn't do it, she'll make the Monsignor reassign Father to the Arans. Me, too!"

"How did the Father react? Is he going to do it?"

"No, he said he would not. Saint Timothy's no place, he said, to air Maude's personal problems."

"Good man!"

"I think so, too, Mrs. Kennedy."

"I know you do, Viola. I've long known of your feelings toward the Father. If that Maude tries to have the two of you reassigned, I'll put a stop to it! I know the Monsignor! And the Bishop!

"Will you tell the other vestry members when we're meeting?"

"I will, Mrs. Kennedy, as soon as the Father approves it. But," she hesitated "please don't tell anyone how I feel about the Father."

"Your secret's safe with me, dear."

Arm-in-arm, the male trio entered the parlor of Saint Timothy's. "Don't forget, chums."

"Wha'?"

"John Long's will be our destination after every vestry meeting, starting today."

"Ladies included, like before," John reminded.

"Pat, are you fully prepared for this meeting?"

"Wha' do you mean?"

"Have you a wee bottle of Jameson's to add to Maude's tea?"

Davis patted a coat pocket. "Of course, I do. We need to maneuver Maude between the two of us at the table."

John touched his beard. "Why's that?"

"Not knowing which side she drinks her tea on, we must sit on either side of 'Her Ladyship."

Pat stepped away from the other two men. "Gotta make sure the tea's being brewed as we asked."

George began pumping the others' hands. "Good luck, lads! We're going to win this one."

"It'll be the best vestry meeting ever," Pat prophesied as he headed for the kitchen.

Father Murphy was stoic but the others of the vestry seemed exuberant, with the exception of Maude Connor. She was angrily resisting being seated by John and Pat between them.

Even the elderly Mrs. Kennedy appeared excited, greeting the others with winks and smiles. Murphy took a chair at the end of the table with Viola and Joyce alongside.

With a nod from Murphy, Joyce announced "The meeting will come to order, please. All members are present." Duty done, she sat down.

Immediately Maude Connor was on her feet. "Father, I want to begin this meeting with an announcement about that scandalous article recently attributed to me, possibly written by an unscrupulous member of this vestry."

Immediately Joyce was on her feet. "Objection, Father. The list of agenda subjects at each chair takes precedence over incidental items, such as Maude's, which can be heard after our scheduled business."

Maude exploded. "Why you...you impertinent gimp! You're not even from this county! Connors have been in Mallow and Cork since before the Normans!"

She appealed to Murphy. "Father, silence this person," she pointed at Joyce. "I have an important announcement to make here and now."

Father Murphy sighed but maintained a smile. "Perhaps it would be better, Maude, if you had the floor at the conclusion of the business items which brought us here."

Grimacing, Maude sat down heavily, reaching for her cup of tea. Pat pushed it toward her so she could more easily reach it. As he did so, he winked at George across the table.

Joyce waved the agenda sheet. "Father, our first item of business is the vestry's selection of Saint Timothy's representative to the executive committee planning the 500th anniversary of Mallow Castle, possibly the most important event of our lifetime.

"I think the necessary qualifications of any nominee for this prestigious position are evident. Our nominee, representing Saint Timothy, must be eminently better qualified than all others.

"You see on the agenda sheet before you," Joyce waved the paper, "a précis of the duties and responsibilities of the chairperson of the committee. On the chairperson's shoulders rests the heavy burden for the success of this celebration. It will be a full-time responsibility, planning and managing the activities of five other community leaders.

"Is here any discussion on the chairperson's duties and responsibilities?" Joyce again surveyed the members.

Father Murphy gestured. "I think you have described the position very well, Joyce, and the necessary qualifications of our nominee."

George slapped his palm on the table. "Hear, hear. Concise but thorough," he bowed toward Joyce.

No one spoke for several moments.

Mrs. Kennedy rose to break the silence. "In my opinion we have among us here the person best qualified to be chairperson of the celebration committee. I nominate Maude Connor to be Saint Timothy's candidate for the position of chairperson. Sacrificing her absence from our church will be difficult but we must gladly make it for the benefit of others."

"Are there any other nominees?"

George stood and pointed toward a pensive Maude Connor, sipping her third cup of tea. "I move we elect Maude Connor by acclamation to be chairperson of the 500th anniversary celebration committee."

Joyce stood again. "Ayes? Nays?"

Everyone except Maude responded 'aye.'

"By acclamation with the exception of our modest nominee, Maude Connor is Saint Timothy's candidate for chairperson of Mallow Castle's anniversary celebration. Congratulations, Maude!"

Urged to her unsteady feet by Pat and John, Connor looked pleased but baffled. "I suppose I must thank you. I will represent Saint Timothy's to the utmost of my abilities."

Joyce took charge again, waving the agenda sheet. "Father, the last scheduled item for today is an announcement from Mrs. Kennedy, which I think may surprise us all."

Kennedy stood again, ignoring Connor sitting across from her. "My announcement is short and simple, Father. I donate this cheque in the amount of E2,000. for whatever use Saint Timothy's may desire. Thank you."

Surprised and delighted, Murphy accepted the cheque and held it up for all to see. "Thank you for this handsome donation, Mrs. Kennedy. I assure you our budget committee will use your donation wisely."

Maude Connor kicked her chair aside as she arose.

Blinking at the others, she turned to Father Murphy. "I see now this was all a stage-play by you people," she swept them a scathing look, "to separate me from the vestry where I have served faithfully for so long."

She stared at Father Murphy. "Even my own priest acceded to this charade!

"You will all regret that you have ridiculed and removed me," she scowled at them. "I was not even allowed to speak in my own defense against that malicious advertisement.

"My generous gift to the Youth Group now appears niggardly in comparison to the donation just made by this woman," she pointed at Kennedy, "who I thought was my friend."

Head held high, Connor marched out of the parlor, slamming the door behind her.

Clasping his hands, Murphy rose from his chair and began a prayer asking for the forgiveness of Connor and themselves.

TWENTY ONE

"Pints all around!" shouted George the moment the six vestry members walked into John Long's. Pat hurried to their favorite table to seat Mrs. Kennedy at the end. John placed Viola across from him, while Pat seated Joyce next to Viola.

"What's the celebration?" Sean asked, unloading his tray with the pints.

Viola was the first to answer "Freedom! Free at last, free at last! Isn't that what Martin Luther King said?"

"Glory! This is like my graduation party from St. Peter's Academy," recalled Mrs. Kennedy, licking the foam from the top of her pint. "I've got this round," she signaled to Sean.

"No, dear lady," Pat waved at Sean. "The gents claim the honor of paying for this liberation celebration."

John stood, pint held high. "A toast to our prowess! We pulled it off! Maud is out of our hair."

"What hair?" joked Pat. "Your pate's as sparse as mine."

Viola laughed at the two, adding, "I wish the Father was here."

"Next time, Viola, next time," George promised. "We gents propose that we get together here after each vestry meeting. Right here at John Long's!"

"Father permitting, maybe we can just meet here and save wear and tear and clean-up of parlor," Joyce grinned.

"Keep an eye on the door, John," Pat advised solemnly. "We don't want 'Her Ladyship' catching us having fun."

"Wouldn't be fun," John objected. "She'd probably roll a hand grenade under our table."

Kennedy nodded. "Maude seemed right perturbed."

"Especially when your donation doubled hers—sans reporter, photographer and front page coverage."

A flushed Viola stood, uncertain of words but sure of her objective.

"We owe a deep debt of gratitude to Father Murphy. He didn't buckle to Maude nor did he allow us to pillory her."

A hush fell over the six at the table as Viola's words were considered.

"Is it, true, Viola, that Maude threatened to make the Monsignor transfer the two of you to the Aran Islands?"

Somber-faced, Viola agreed. "That's what she said."

"I suggest," Pat said, looking at the others, "that you compose a strong letter to the Bishop stating what a spiritual leader, dah, dah, dah—you know the right words, Viola—the Father is and how valuable he is to Saint Timothy's, our city and county. Maybe such a letter would dissuade the Monsignor from Maude's attempt to reassign the Father and you."

"We should all sign it," Kennedy spoke, still trying to coax Sean to hand her the tab.

"Here," Joyce offered her steno pad to Viola. "Let's draft it right now while we're all here."

Viola hesitated. "I've never written a bishop before. I don't know where to start."

Mrs. Kennedy patted her on the arm. "You're a capable young woman capable of anything she puts her mind to including…" She winked, failing to finish the sentence.

Guessing how Kennedy would have completed the thought, Viola blushed.

"Sure you're our best writer," George and John exclaimed, both patting her shoulder.

"Here's my pen," Pat offered. "How do we start it?"

Viola spoke as she began writing. "To the Most Reverend Howard Hagen, Bishop of Cork and Ross. Cathedral of Saint Mary and Saint Anne, Cork."

Everyone smiled at the good start.

"We the undersigned members of the vestry of Saint Timothy's, Mallow, beg your indulgence to describe to your Excellency the outstanding pastoral services provided us by Father Aloysis T. Murphy, S.J., rector of Saint Timothy's..."

She looked about the faces surrounding her at the pint-laden table at John Long's. "Is that too wordy?"

"A splendid start!" was their loud answer.

She began writing, then reading aloud for their approval.

"Father Murphy faithfully observes the charges given Saint Timothy by Saint Paul.

'Fight well in the Lord's battles. Cling tightly to your faith. Always keep your conscience clear, doing what you know is right."

She stopped. "Am I correctly quoting that? My memory isn't always reliable and we want this to be perfect for the Father's sake. Right?"

Mrs. Kennedy wagged her hand. "Your memory is exactly correct, Viola. It's a perfect beginning."

Following Kennedy's example, John raised his hand. "Let's put something in there about his grand care of his parishioners. How he visits the sick and troubled, like me and the missus when I got caught in the hay bailer."

Joyce spoke up. "And how he's always available, even comes to our homes, to help us along during the rough places."

John's hand was in the air again. "Like the time those EU restrictions put lots of farmers out of work."

There was so many cited examples that Viola often had to slow down the barrage. "Say that again, Pat. I didn't catch it all."

By the time two more rounds of drinks were consumed, the draft letter to the Bishop extolling Father Murphy's performance of duties was finished.

Kennedy was uncommonly exuberant. "Now, let's all go over to your office, Viola, and you prepare the final letter on your processor."

Toasting Viola's effort, George added "We'll all sign it and away it goes to the Cathedral in Cork!"

"I'll take it to *An Post* and mail it right away! We don't want to lose our fine priest to the whim of 'Her Ladyship.'"

Joyce cautioned. "Maybe there should be a post script saying Father Murphy has no knowledge—nor will we tell him—of this letter. I know you can word it just right, Viola."

Bar bills paid, the six vestry members marched across the street to Viola's office, after she made certain Father Murphy was nowhere about to notice their activity.

In Kinsale the day was not going smoothly for Joe. He'd just received E300. from Timothy Evers of the Temple of the Augury for Joe's map and list of the interior dimensions of the Church of Saint Timothy.

Cherie, waiting for him in the SUV driver's seat, thrust out her hand for the envelope of money as he approached. "What'd he say?"

Joe spit. "He said he wished he'd hired a professional to do the job. Said my figures were amateurish and approximate."

He walked around to get in the passenger door when Cherie pumped the accelerator and left him behind in a swirl of dust. She stuck a hand out the driver's window, waving goodbye.

Thinking it was a joke, Joe sat down on the kerb to wait Cherie's laughing return with the SUV and money.

He checked his watch. Two minutes had elapsed, then five. She should have returned by now, he kept thinking. A terrible suspicion grew, transforming his expression.

Gradually he accepted that Cherie's hand wave was the last he might ever see of her and the SUV. "I'll bash her smart face," he muttered, closing and opening his fist.

"She left me flat, taking the vehicle and all the money," he shouted. Soon the anger turned to gasps and tears.

Evers stepped out of the Temple just then and, seeing Joe sitting on the kerb, approached. "What's wrong, Joe? Where's the SUV?"

Sniveling, Joe wiped his eyes with a hand. "Just comin' to see you, sir. The vehicle was gone when I came outside. Someone stole it right from under my nose."

"You're serious?"

"Yes, sir." Tears began again. "I'm stranded here. Maybe you'd better call the police."

"Come in, Joe," Evers beaconed. "I'll telephone them right now. They're sure to want a statement from you. After that maybe they'll give you a ride to the bus depot in Cork."

It was ten p.m. when the police dropped Joe at the Cork bus station. Disconsolate and without bus fare, he sat in the waiting room, hoping to catch a free ride home to Mallow.

"As if I have a home anywhere now," he cursed, stepping

outside the depot and walking north along the secondary national route to Mallow.

Luckily, he had walked no more than five minutes when a battered Nissan pickup pulled over at his signal and he crawled in beside a grizzled farmer.

"Out for a late night walk, are you?" The elderly driver lit his pipe with one hand while studying Joe. "No, I haven't any money if you wuz thinkin' of asking or takin'."

"No, sir. All I want is to get home tonight."

"Where might that be?"

"Mallow, sir. Could you give me a ride there?"

The driver lit the pipe again, puffing harder. "Nope, sorry. Halfway's my home and I've got to stop there. My best heifer's calving right about now."

After being dropped at the Halfway House turnoff, Joe tried alternately walking and flagging down other cars. A string of several vehicle lights behind him made him turn and try signaling again.

The last car was a big one, probably a Mercedes, he guessed as he turned and waved even harder. Before facing its blinding headlights, he recognized it as a Mercedes.

The headlights were his next-to-last remembrance as the big black vehicle struck him.

His last fleeting memory was that the Mercedes was slowing to help, but then increased speed, leaving him bloody and broken, lying beside the road.

Two days later, Joe was awakened by the sound of rustling sheets. A nurse eyed him as she replaced a white sheet over his spread-eagled body in a hospital bed. She called to someone over her shoulder. "He's awake now, Doctor."

Joe moaned as he looked about. Both his legs were in traction above the bed in a v-shape. His arms were splayed apart overhead behind him. Arms and legs were held immobile in plaster casts. His body looked like a big X, with only his head and trunk in the middle.

A middle-aged man dressed in white bent over him, studying his pupils with a bright light.

"God!" Joe gasped. "Am I dead?"

The man chuckled. "That question just graduated you from critical to serious," he turned to jot a note on a clip board. "And recovering nicely despite several serious injuries," he added, smiling at Joe.

"Good to see you awake at last. You had me worried."

Despite a foul taste and dry mouth, Joe managed to croak. "Are you a doctor? Where am I?"

The doctor nodded. "I'm Doctor Connelly and this is the Mallow Hospital. Do you feel good enough to be questioned by the police about your accident?"

The dry mouth prevented an answer until the nurse held a straw and water glass to his lips. He felt terrified by the mention of police.

"Am I in trouble? I don't want to talk to any police."

A thermometer in the mouth stopped his speaking for a minute. "They want to know who hit you on the highway," the nurse explained. "Hit and run is a serious crime. That's what they want to ask you about."

"I don't know who hit me!" Joe panicked. "All I remember was this big black Mercedes coming at me!"

"What's your name?"

"Joe."

"Okay, Joe. Just relax. I'm giving you a sedative to let you sleep a bit more. The police can wait until you're better."

TWENTY TWO

Something extraordinary was happening. Viola read it in the ashen color of Mrs. Casey's habitually stoic face. She opened Viola's door without knocking, itself an aberration.

Mrs. Casey pointed toward the front door. "He's here! The Bishop's here!"

Disbelieving, Viola bolted from her chair and to the church front. Just climbing the steps was the Most Reverend Howard Hagen, Bishop of Cork and Ross. He tipped his black fedora as a breathless Viola bowed.

"Welcome to Saint Timothy's, Excellency," she gasped, unsure if she should extend her hand. "I'm Viola Norton, Father Murphy's administrator."

"And where is the good Father Murphy, Miss Norton? I understand your surprise. That's exactly what I wanted this short visit to be…a surprise."

"And a happy one, Excellency," Viola followed through seamlessly. "Father Murphy is praying, probably in his favorite place yonder in the front pew. Won't you please come this way?"

Viola paused as they entered the church. "Excellency, this is Mrs. Casey, our housekeeper. The Bishop, Mrs. Casey," she added needlessly as Casey repeatedly bowed.

Inside, the Bishop raised his finger to his lips as he walked down the main aisle toward Murphy's lone figure, on his knees in the front pew.

Still silent, the Bishop genuflected and nudged Murphy over a space, then knelt beside him.

Eyes open, Murphy looked to see who his companion was.

He shot up off the kneeler. "Your Excellency," he stammered. "What a surprise! Welcome to Saint Timothy's!" He kissed the bishop's ring.

"Sit, down, Father," the Bishop grinned. "Finish your prayers, then we'll talk in your office."

Later, Mrs. Casey proudly served tea in the manse's best china to the two men in Murphy's small office. Viola stood on the other side of the door, listening and holding a notepad.

Murphy raised his cup. "Your health, Excellency."

"Know why I'm here, Father?" The Bishop slowly tasted, then set cup and saucer on the tray.

"I can only surmise that you're here to relieve me, Excellency." Murphy braced for the bad news. On the other side of the door, Viola caught her breath and crossed herself at Murphy's words.

Chuckling, the Bishop took another sip. "Far from it, Father. I'm here to challenge, not chastise you."

"How may I serve you, Excellency?"

"Father, I want you to prepare a plan to receive and train newly ordained priests in our diocese. I want you to show them the down-to-earth things a young priest needs to know about how to become a true shepherd to his flock. I find those are topics our seminaries overlook in their haste to produce us new priests.

"It's come to my attention that you are performing an outstanding job here at Saint Timothy's. I want you to share your expertise in the caring and love of parishioners with the newly-ordained. Will you consider it?"

"I'd do my best to meet your challenge, Excellency.

Not to digress, but we would be honored to have you for luncheon today in the manse."

"Oh, no, thanks. Unfortunately I must be in Fermoy in two hours. I apologize for the surprise and shortness of my visit with you. I do have a request to make, another surprise, I fear."

"Certainly, Excellency. What may we do?"

He finished his tea. "My request is a most unusual one. I'd like a few minutes with your vestry before I depart. Here are their names," he handed Murphy a list.

"Perhaps these individuals—only these—could meet with me privately in the parlor before I leave for Fermoy?"

Viola opened the closed door and took the list of names before Murphy could ask for assistance. "I'll call them now, Father. They'll be in the parlor in fifteen minutes."

The Bishop looked at Murphy as he sat back down. "Now that's what I call an efficient administrator, Father. That young lady's a prize!"

"Thank you, Excellency. I couldn't agree with you more. Neither Saint Timothy's nor I could do without her."

Less than an hour later, Viola had the six vestry members excitedly talking in the parlor about meeting Bishop Hagen. She scolded them for their noise then left for Murphy's office to bring the Bishop.

"This way, Excellency."

Hand on the door, she stopped Murphy from following. "You're not invited, Father. Just the Bishop and vestry, he said."

Puzzled, Murphy exhaled and sat back down at his desk.

"Ladies and gentlemen," Viola announced as they

entered the parlor, "the Most Reverend Howard Hagen, Bishop of Cork and Ross."

In turn she introduced each of the others, beginning with Mrs. Kennedy. "Please be seated." Hagen smiled broadly.

"Thank you for coming on such short notice. I intend to take only a minute or so of your time to say thank you for your thoughtful letter about the faithfulness and diligence of Father Murphy," he pointed over his shoulder to Murphy's closed door.

"It is a delight—and I might add, a rather seldom one— to hear such a good report on our pastors.

"Since your letter seemed a bit fearful, I wanted to come here and assure you that there are no plans to transfer Father Murphy from Saint Timothy's. To the contrary, I have given him the genesis of an important additional duty I want him to implement at Saint Timothy's for the benefit of the entire diocese.

"I apologize to you, as I did to Father Murphy," he turned to Viola, "and to your very capable parish administrator for the shortness of this visit. But I must depart now to make a previous appointment in Fermoy which I am unable to change or cancel.

"Farewell, faithful vestry members. Please remember your bishop and our diocese in your prayers. Thank you." He blessed them and left the parlor with Viola.

She escorted Hagen back to the waiting sedan and driver. Father Murphy stood by the open car door.

"Goodbye to you, Miss Norton. Goodbye, Father. I'd appreciate any thoughts you have after considering the challenge I've issued you. Next visit, I'll spend a day or two if convenient to you and Saint Timothy's."

A wave and the Bishop rode away in his big black sedan.

"Whew!" Viola and Murphy exclaimed together and then laughed. "Is the vestry still here?" he asked.

"They are, Father, enjoying Mrs. Casey's tea and biscuits to spoil their lunches."

"Let's join them, Viola." Murphy was excited. "Then you can tell me what this whirlwind visit was really about."

"Haven't you heard of the strict rule of confidentiality?" she quipped, giggling at his expression.

TWENTY THREE

"Time for your medicine, Joe," the nurse trilled in his ear and handed him a cup.

He blinked, looking above him at the harsh white light. "The police are here again, Joe," she took back the empty cup "insisting on seeing you. Doctor Connelly feels you are sufficiently recovered for a short ten minute interview."

He moaned pitifully. "When can I get out of this harness and go home?"

"That's a long time off, the doctor says. You must stay completely immobile and let those bones knit."

Suddenly the door was filled by two figures, one male wearing a suit and a female in the blue-uniform of the *Garda*. "I'm Inspector O'Bryan and this is Constable Fannon who will record our conversation. Have you any objection?" O'Bryan said as he sat in a chair next to the female constable, already taking notes.

Joe shook his head but said nothing.

"I understand you have no objection to the recording of our conversation here," the inspector said for the record Constable Fannon was making.

O'Bryan cleared his throat. "The first matter is your identity. The hospital has no record and there were absolutely no identity papers on you when admitted.

"Who are you and where is your residence?"

Joe shrugged. "Everyone here calls me 'Joe' so I guess that's my name. I cannot remember any other. My head hurts."

"You claim amnesia? The doctor says you might have a slight concussion. You'd better not refuse to identify yourself to a police officer. I warn you, that in itself, is a felony. I ask again, what is your name and residence?"

Joe shrugged, helplessly. "I don't know. I wish I did."

Pensive, O'Bryan moved on to another question. "Tell me about the accident which caused you to be here, Joe."

"Aye. I remember walking out of the Cork bus depot and looking for a ride north since I was broke."

O'Bryan nodded. He already had a statement from the depot clerk who remembered Joe. "Then what?"

"I started walking along the road and finally caught a ride with a farmer who dropped me off at Halfway."

O'Bryan nodded again. He also had the farmer's statement. "And then?"

"I started walking again toward Mallow when several cars came up behind me and I began signaling for a ride. They speeded by me anyway.

"Except for a big, black car in the very rear. It was a one of those expensive German cars, a Mercedes."

Joe began perspiring so much that the nurse wiped his brow with a tissue. "Thanks."

"Please continue, Joe."

"I remember wagging my arm at the Mercedes but it didn't slow down. Instead it came directly at me and hit me. It struck me real solid and I went down in a heap. I was hurt bad. I was bleeding all over the pavement."

"Were you able to see a license plate on the car?"

"Are you kiddin'?" Joe tried to shift his position but failed and moaned. "I was hurt real bad," he repeated angrily.

"You're sure it was a black Mercedes?"

Angrier than ever, Joe yelled. "Yes, just like I said!"

The nurse checked his blood pressure and summoned

the doctor from the hallway. "Stop the interview," the doctor said. "You've upset the patient and you must go."

"Just one quick question, please," O'Bryan pleaded. "What do you remember next, Joe?"

Breathing heavily into the just-applied oxygen mask, Joe shut his eyes at the memory. "The Mercedes was slowing down to help me, I thought. But then it speeded up and took off to the north as if the devil wuz after it!"

On their way back to the police station, O'Bryan gave several orders to the constable note-taker. "Check our vehicle people and see if there are any black Mercedes registered in the county, If so, whose are they? Also check with missing persons to see if there's anyone loose who fits Joe's description.

"Who the hell is he?" O'Bryan cracked his knuckles in frustration. "Send someone to take his prints tomorrow!"

The headline of Mallow's usually staid *An Post* newspaper doubled the sale of the paper before noon.

MAN STRUCK BY HIT AND RUN
IN CRITICAL CONDITION

A man yet to be identified by Police, but believed to be 25-30 years of age, was struck and seriously injured on the N20 by a dark sedan which immediately left the scene without giving aid, according to a Police spokesman. The accident occurred Tuesday night around 11:30 p.m. near Halfway House, six miles south of Mallow.

"The Garda is working full time," said Inspector T.H. O'Bryan of the Mallow Police. "We are attempting to identify both the victim of this heinous accident and the driver of the vehicle which struck him. Hit and run, compounded by failure to stop and aid is a major crime. Anyone who saw or has any knowledge of this crime should immediately contact the Police at 666-111."

O'Bryan leaned back in his chair that morning, wishing he were home and in bed. He'd been up all night, alternately drinking coffee and gathering tidbits of data about the hit and run accident on national route N20. At 9:00 he briefed the Superintendent but that went badly due to the dearth of available information at that hour.

Constable Fannon knocked and he waved her in, hoping she brought good news.

"Sir, none of the missing persons listed in the central registry match the physical descriptions of Joe," she waved a photo of Joe taken in the hospital. "His prints were lifted this morning, but no match there yet, either."

O'Bryan's scowl deepened.

Fannon raised one finger for encouragement. "The Central Authority reports there is only one Mercedes registered in the Mallow area. Could that be our hit and run vehicle, sir?"

The inspector jumped from his chair and grabbed Constable Fannon for a quick jig around his desk. Slowing, he loosed her long enough to issue more instructions.

"Get me an investigator in here! No, two of 'em! I want that Mercedes impounded and examined by forensics.

And the driver of the car identified and brought here for questioning. On to it!"

He needn't have shouted. Freed, Fannon was already out the door.

"Did you ever notice?" Amos, the sexton of Saint Timothy's pointed at the confessional stall halfway down the west aisle of the church. Viola and Mrs. Casey turned and followed his finger.

"The confessional?" Viola asked. "Something wrong with it, too?" The three of them had been inspecting the church interior for cleanliness before matins.

"No, just never saw one made like that," Amos dusted the top and sides of the stall. "I remember as a kid that they all had a little door in the rear for the priest to sit and two open sides where us folks knelt.

"This one," he pointed again, "has a center door leading to a closed box for the penitent while the priest sits on either side of the box, in the open."

Both Casey and Viola shrugged. "Never noticed that before. But guess that's how it was designed when Saint Timothy's was built."

Viola was curious. "What do you make of it, Amos?"

Amos hunched his shoulders. "Dunno, just thought it strange. Seems backwards to me." He began dusting stained glass window sills beside the confessional box.

TWENTY FOUR

Eric Summers was beneath the carriage, removing the oil drain plug when he felt a kick on his leg and a guttural "Come out from under there!"

"Who's that? What do you want?"

"The police, that's who! Get out or I'll drag you out!"

Summers wriggled out from under the Mercedes E-class and stared at the policemen above him.

With a sinking feeling, he repeated, "What do you want?"

"Stand up!"

"Why? Am I being arrested? What for?"

"I can tell by your looks, you know damn well why we're here, Eric Summers. That's your name?"

"Yes. Oh, God! I *am* being arrested!"

"No, just apprehended for questioning down at the station. But if you like, *Mr.* Summers," the older policeman chuckled, "I'll be happy to arrest and cuff you."

"I have to tell my employer where I'm going."

The policeman checked his notebook. "You mean 'Her Ladyship?" He laughed before correcting himself. "I mean Mrs. Maude Connor, of course. We'll inform her. She's coming, too, but separate from you."

At the station, Summers sat in an interview room while a skinny constable stood by the door.

"Ain't I entitled to a solicitor or somethin'?"

Upon entering, Inspector O'Bryan heard the question and answered. "Of course you are, but you're not accused of anything. This is just a routine questioning. Do you want to hire a solicitor to sit here with you?"

"Coffee or tea?" O'Bryan offered before Summers could answer.

"No thanks."

"Mind if our conversation is recorded?' O'Bryan placed a small recorder on the table.

"Guess not, since I'm not arrested or anything."

"Full name and address?"

Summers dutifully provided the information.

"Have you a commercial license to operate a motor vehicle?"

"Yes, sir."

"Where were you Tuesday night at approximately 11:30?"

Beginning to pale, Summers asked "May I have a drink of water?"

The inspector nodded and the constable left the room.

"Where were you, Mr. Summers, at approximately 11:30 hours Tuesday night?"

Summers gulped the water and held the plastic cup out for more. "I was driving Mrs. Connor home from Cork."

"Did you see anything unusual on the N20 on your way home from Cork?"

Summers blinked and studied his hands. "No, sir."

"Did you witness an accident on N20 last night?"

Looking at his hands again, he almost stammered. "No, sir."

"Has the car you were driving last night been in an accident lately?"

"Nothing major, just a paint scrape or two. The car's almost new."

"Other than you, who drives the Mercedes?"

"No one, sir."

"Mrs. Connor was your only passenger?"

"Yes, sir."

"Seated in the back seat or with you in the front?"

"She always rides in the rear, sir. May I call home? My wife expects me home directly from work."

O'Bryan stared at Summers. "What did Mrs. Connor tell you to say about the return trip that night?"

"Well…nothing, sir."

Constable Fannon entered with a single sheet of paper for O'Bryan who glanced at it, then slowly read it in its entirety.

Looking directly at Summers, the inspector cleared his throat. "Mr. Eric Summers I place you under arrest for suspicion of causing and not reporting a serious auto accident on the N20 last night. You will be held here until our investigation of this matter is completed. Yes, you may call a solicitor to meet with you at your earliest convenience."

Motioning to the constable by the door, he said "Take him to the booking desk."

To Constable Fannon, O'Bryan grinned. "Go home and get some rest. See you bright and early in the morning."

"What about that Mrs. Connor, sir?"

"Ah, that bird has flown already. She called the district court judge and demanded to be released on her own recognizance. She'll be back tomorrow for questioning."

Fannon grinned. "Bet she has a good story by then, sir."

"She'd better. This report here," he returned it to her, "is deadly. Good job!"

"Good night, sir."

Eric Summers awoke on a hard cot with the feeling that

he had dreamed badly all night. A cup of jail coffee failed to cheer as he was hustled out of the cell and back to the interrogation room.

Inspector O'Bryan pointed to a chair and Summers sat. Without preamble, the inspector began. "Our conversation is being recorded as it was last night.

"You said last night the Mercedes had not been involved in a recent accident, correct?"

Closing his eyes, Summers nodded.

"Speak up."

"Yes, sir. Just a few paint scratches as I recall."

"Forensics reports your car suffered recent major damage, as recent as last night. That's approximately when there was a serious accident on N20 between a big black car, like yours, and a pedestrian."

Summers shook his head, unable to respond.

"Tell me about the accident, Mr. Summers. You'll feel much better. Were you alert? Maybe had a pint or two in Cork while waiting on Mrs. Connor?"

Summers shook his head. "I didn't have nothin' alcoholic to drink yesterday, Inspector. I'm a good driver. No accidents since I got my commercial ticket."

"Are you aware, Summers, that you struck a pedestrian walking beside the road last night?"

Summers was looking wildly about the small room as if seeking to escape.

O'Bryan snorted. "So far you may be charged with reckless driving, hitting a pedestrian, failing to render assistance, leaving the scene of an accident and withholding evidence. If the pedestrian dies, you could be charged with manslaughter as well."

O'Bryan leaned back in his chair. "Enough, Mr. Summers. Tell me what really happened on your way home from Cork last night. Your sentence might be less severe if you tell me the truth. This is your chance to come clean. NOW!"

"I think I'm going to gawk! Let me outta' here!"

In response, the skinny constable pushed a bucket toward Summers's feet.

"Get him another water, please."

Summers cradled his head in his hands on the table. Tearful, he raised his face. "I'm a married man with a family to support. What was I to do? I had to do what she said or I'd be outa' job!"

"What did Mrs. Connor tell you to do?"

Summers blew his nose with a tissue from the desk. "I started to pull over when we hit the guy on the road. She said 'Don't stop! Speed up!' and called me a gom.

"I wanted to stop and help him, I really did. But I had to do what she said!"

O'Bryan pointed at the door and the constable returned the weeping Summers to his cell.

Maude Connor was escorted into the interrogation room by Constable Fannon who remained standing by the door.

"Have a chair, Mrs. Connor." O'Bryan said to the tight-lipped, scowling female.

"I'm Inspector O'Bryan…"

"Yes, I know your people," Connor interrupted. "As you may know, my family, the Connors, founded the city of Mallow."

"Here to ask you about the accident," O'Bryan ignored her history lesson, "occurring last night on the N20 at approximately 11:30 p.m. in which your vehicle struck a pedestrian beside the road."

"My solicitor advises me to remain silent except for this statement concerning the incident."

"*Incident*?" O'Bryan no longer smiled. "A man was seriously injured and could have died on the spot!"

Glaring, Connor silently passed a paper to the inspector.

O'Bryan put on his glasses, took the paper and began reading it aloud.

"I have no knowledge of any accident last night. On my return home from Cork City, I fell asleep in the rear seat of my automobile, not awakening until arriving at my home, Manor House, Mallow.

(signed) Mrs. Maude S. Connor."

"You understand, Mrs. Connor, that this statement may be used in any subsequent hearing about the accident involving your vehicle striking and injuring another person? Do you further understand you may be questioned under oath about it and any other evidence brought to the court's attention?"

Another glare was the only answer as Connor left the room, slamming the door behind her.

"It's that Inspector O'Bryan again, Father," Viola called through the open door separating their offices.

"Good morning, Inspector. Father Brown speaking."

"More sticky business for you, Father, from your

parishioners. You asked that I call you when one of them was in trouble."

"Thank you, Inspector. Who is it?"

O'Bryan lit a pipe and puffed strenuously. "Not one, but two souls, Father. Mrs. Connor and her driver, Eric Summers."

"Must have been an auto accident," Murphy guessed.

"Exactly. Summers is in jail here awaiting possible trial. Madame Connor, aka 'Her Ladyship,' was ordered released on her own recognizance. I thought you might like to visit Summers. He seems so depressed that we initiated a suicide watch."

"Thanks for your call, Inspector. I'll be right over as soon as I air-up my bicycle tires."

TWENTY FIVE

Locking his 'High Nelly' bike in a rack, Murphy entered the police station and was escorted directly to the Summers cell by a constable who stood outside watching them.

"Hello, Eric. How are you?"

"Doing the best I can, Father, under the circumstances. Thank you for coming to see me."

Following Murphy's example, Summers sat beside him on the cot. "Have you heard from my wife, Father? I'm worried she might do something foolish 'cause I'm in the lock-up."

"I called her right before I left the church, Eric. She sounded normal, but very worried about you."

"Wouldn't have a cigarette, would you, Father?"

"No, I don't. Like me to bring you a carton when I return?"

"Thanks, Father. Being in here I should quit smoking and save money. I've probably lost my job if I'm asked to testify about what happened."

"That's possible," Murphy nodded. "Now do you want to tell me what this is all about? If you'd rather not, that's alright, too."

Summers took a deep breath. "I'd like to tell you about it, Father. I need your advice now more than ever. You probably remember that time I squandered my paycheck on the horses."

The two men looked at each other for a moment, before Summers spoke. "Well, here's what happened. I took Mrs. Connor to Cork yesterday and brought her back home last night. The police tell me it was around 11:30 when I hit a pedestrian standing on the side of the road.

"The police asked if I'd been drinking yesterday and I said no. The night was real dark and the guy I hit was wearing black clothing of some kind. I couldn't see him, truly.

"I couldn't avoid him, Father! Believe me, I slammed on the brakes but there he was, too close to the car. I am very, very sorry that I hurt him. Don't even know his name, the police wouldn't say."

Murphy nodded, encouraging him to continue.

"There's is one thing in my favor, Father."

"What is it, Eric?"

"I tried to stop and help the poor guy but Mrs. Connor yelled at me to keep going. She even ordered me to speed up!"

Summers held his head. "So l did as she told me…like a fool. Now I'm in jail, out of a steady job, and she's probably sitting in the Manor House laughing her head off over tea and cakes.

"Is there anything you can do to help me, Father?"

"Is what you just said the truth, the entire, unblemished truth?"

"Yes, Father. It's all true."

"Eric, I'm unsure how I can help you with the police but I know what will aid you otherwise."

"What is it? Whatever it is, I'll do it!"

Murphy stood, waving the constable away from the window, pulled the thin purple stole from his pocket, kissed and donned it.

Understanding, Summers knelt in front of Murphy, crossed himself and began. "Bless me, Father, for I have sinned…"

An hour later, Murphy sat at his office desk, thinking about what Summers had confessed. Murphy believed Eric had been truthful. He grappled with the thought of his duty to both of his Saint Timothy communicants. In good conscience, how could he—their priest— believe one and not the other?

Horrified, Eunice dropped the plate of her mistress' favorite marmalade. Crash! It broke on the floor, spatters of apricot staining the carpet. Eunice crossed herself, certain of immediate dismissal.

Maude Connor didn't notice. She stood at the head of the long dining table, waving the morning edition of *An Post*.

"I'll sue that lying, fabricating little editor for everything he's got…and more!

"Look at that headline!" Connor shouted. "He's impugning my reputation! He won't get away with this!"

Striding from the dining room, Connor stopped at the nearest telephone to ring her solicitor. "Come at once!" she ordered the solicitor who was probably reading the same headline and anticipating her angry call.

VICTIN STILL CRITICAL;
HIT AND RUN VEHICLE ID'D

According to a police internal report obtained by the An Post, the vehicle involved in the hit and run of a pedestrian on N20 south of Mallow night before last belongs to a local resident. The vehicle is said to be a black Mercedes sedan.

The police refuse to identify the resident until their investigation of the accident is completed. The injured, still unnamed victim, is described by hospital personnel as a male in his twenties, of average build and with black hair. He remains in the Critical Care Ward of the Mallow Hospital with several broken limbs, a concussion and internal injuries.

Inspector O'Bryan stood outside his door, drinking coffee with Constable Fannon as he saw Father Murphy approaching. Without a word, he gestured Murphy inside.

"I'm sure I know the subject. Father."

Murphy blurted, "Do you believe Summers's account of the accident?"

"I do."

"Including that Mrs. Connor ordered him not to stop to help, instead told him to keep going and speed up?"

"Ahh, Father, that's the rub. We have contrasting statements from the only two eye witnesses. The public prosecutor is unhappy, not knowing which person a jury might believe."

Murphy agreed. "One is the town's wealthy and respected dowager, the other a poor driver with family.

Seems to me a jury would side with the driver who admits he struck the pedestrian. I believe him, don't you?"

"There you go again, Father. It's not my place to judge the case before trial, which there's sure to be. Why don't you meet with Mrs. Connor and determine for yourself if her statement—that she was conveniently asleep all the way back to Mallow—is true?"

Murphy felt for a pipe, stopped, recalling he'd left it at the church. "Inspector, you'd say I was again interfering with an official police investigation."

"We both seek truth and justice, Father."

Murphy studied the other man. "And faith, Inspector. Don't forget faith."

TWENTY SIX

Although the daylight was long gone from Rafferty Street, the John Long Bar was aglow with bright lights and high spirits. At their favorite table facing the end of the long bar sat the three Saint Timothy vestrymen. They had just finished a dart toss for the next round of drinks. John won.

He sat contently waiting his free pint while glancing at the bar's copy of the morning news. "Did ya' see this bitty story about the auto that did the hit and run the other night?"

"No, what about it?" Pat and George asked in unison.

"Sez here," John pointed to the article, "that the vehicle was a black Mercedes belonging to a local."

Pat jerked to full attention. "That can only be Maude Connor! She's got a big Mercedes."

"No other," George intoned. "Has to be 'Her Ladyship.' She's the guilty one, eh? She left the poor bloody man there, lying on the pavement of the N20 without stopping to help!"

"She should be charged and prosecuted, just like we'd be!" John banged his glass.

"Bet she'll never even be charged. That one!"

Pat drained his pint. "Unless we," he studied his chums, "do something to bring her guilt to the public's attention."

Looking at each other, John finally said, "Like what?" "We can run an advertisement tellin' everyone who owns that Mercedes vehicle.

"Don't sign it or she'll sue us for somethin'," Pat offered.

"Let's drape her front gate with bandages."

"Nah, what would that prove?"

"How about this?" Pat lifted three fingers to Sean, the barman, for another round.

"Her car must at the police shop being photographed for evidence. Once they're done with it, we—gents that we are—volunteer to drive it back to Manor House for her. Saves the police a trip.

"On the way there, we stop and paint red crosses on the car doors and a big **DANGER** sign on its front. We park it in front of Saint Timothy's where everyone sees it, knows it's hers and that it was the hit and run auto.

"And we walk away as innocent as can be," George added. "I like it."

Viola, usually calm and collected, was upset. Father Murphy had hardly touched a meager breakfast of oatmeal, dry toast and coffee. Here it was, going on noon, and she searched for him, guessing he was probably in the first pew of the chapel.

Last night Viola dreamed that Father Murphy had a fever. In the dream, she couldn't decide whether to call a doctor or simply feel his forehead.

How would he react to her touch?

This morning, she still had no answer although the dream had kept her uneasy all night.

She found him in his usual place, kneeling in the pew and praying in a low voice. Did he ever mention her in his long prayers?

Hoping to overhear, she bowed and entered the pew, kneeling beside him. His proximity alongside her made her tingle. She leaned closer to catch his low words.

"Let me not lose faith in other people," he murmured.

"Preserve me from minding little stings or giving them,

"Open wide the eyes of my soul that I may see good in all things,

"Grant me this day some new vision of thy truth…"

A slight movement alerted him to her presence. His eyes widened in surprise, seeing her so close.

"Sorry to disturb you, Father," she crossed herself and turned to him. "This may be an inopportune time and place for my request."

"Dear Viola," he smiled, patting her hand. "What may I do for you?"

The touch of his hand was so electrifying, she almost forgot to respond.

"Father, when eventually you are transferred to the diocese in Cork, please ask that I be reassigned there with you."

Murphy chuckled. "Whatever makes you think that I might be worthy to serve in the diocese? Why, I imagined the other day that the Bishop was here to give me my walking papers."

"No, Father. The Bishop wasn't here to just say 'hello and God bless.'"

"Then why?"

"He came to acknowledge a letter sent him by your vestry. We wrote him that you are an exceptional pastor whom we love and want to keep with us as long as possible."

Murphy lowered his head to the rail. "I'm overwhelmed by your words."

Finally, he looked at her. "But I aim to be a faithful pastor to you and others, not just a popular one."

She stood up. "I know, Father. Please don't forget to

take me with you. Now, let's go to lunch before Mrs. Casey becomes grouchy."

Later Viola knocked on Murphy's door again, gesturing. "Father, I think you should come."

"What's wrong?"

"There's a big car parked in front of the church with some signs on it. A photographer from the *Journal* is out there taking pictures of it for some reason."

Outside a few people had gathered, gawking at a black Mercedes parked in front of the church. On the sides of the car had been painted symbols of the ambulance service.

The front of the auto was hidden by a large white and black homemade sign reading **DANGER!**

"What's this all about?" Murphy asked the photographer.

"Dunno, Father. The editor told me to get over here right away and take a shot of this car in front of your church. It must be the one mentioned in the paper yesterday. It's the hit and run vehicle and belongs to that Mrs. Connor over at Manor House. I guess my editor thinks the photo deserves an article in the morning paper.

"Shall I get a shot of you standing by the car, Father?"

"Absolutely not! Saint Timothy's has no connection to that accident. Please emphasize that to your editor."

"Prior planning prevents poor performance," Maude Connor cackled to herself as she planned the next day's 'program,' as she called it.

First, was the guest list. Second, a special luncheon menu must emphasize the hospitality and elegance of her home, stately old Manor House. Next she must carefully pair bridge partners among the three important ladies being invited for luncheon.

Lastly, she must practice a few discreet talking points her guests would not only remember but would take home with them to discuss with their husbands and associates.

"If this succeeds," she gloated aloud, "it's my 'Stay Out of Court' card!" She devoted the rest of the day adding details to her ambitious plans.

Maude's close friend, Amelia Carter, was the first to appear at the Manor House door the next morning at 11:30. Amelia was not only a friend but a confidante. Maude had already provided Amelia copies of newspaper articles as background for the discussions she wanted Amelia to initiate during the 'program.'

The next arrival was Mary Barnes, wife of Mallow's leading solicitor, perhaps Maude's expensive defender if she needed counsel.

Last to arrive in a long, polished Bentley sedan was Margaret Kenelly, wife of the presiding judge of the District Court of Mallow. Margaret hopefully would repeat Maude's talking points to her honorable justice/husband who would quash—if it came to that—Maude's appearance in his court.

Maude rang the bell for Eunice to serve a light tea to ladies while they gathered before the sumptuous luncheon being prepared since early morning. After the usual desultory chatting, Maude escorted her guests into the dining room, set with her best polished silver, china and linen.

The seating had been as carefully planned as the menu. Margaret Kenelly sat opposite Maude, as they would partner at bridge later. Amelia and Mary sat at Maude's side.

As planned, Amelia started the after-dessert conversation. "I read the most interesting article in the newspaper recently about that accident on the N20, Maude. I believe you saw the accident?"

"No," Maude began serenely. "That article was entirely inaccurate, Amelia. I had fallen asleep in the rear of the car on the way home after a tiring day in Cork City. I was unaware of the accident until I read about it, as you must have, in the morning paper."

Their conversation about the accident continued to the bridge table after dessert and coffee. "How extraordinary," Margaret Kenelly exclaimed. "And how fortunate that you were not injured, my dear. I understand that a pedestrian was struck by the auto and suffered several broken bones." She opened the bidding with one diamond.

Maude nodded sagely. "So I've heard. My driver has been questioned by the police. Since he's been absent from his duties since the accident, I presume they are holding and may charge him." Maude raised two diamonds when her turn came.

"How terrible for you, Maude, having to do without a chauffer all this time."

Mary doubled the diamonds.

"Thank you, Mary. We Connors are used to adversity." Maude bid two hearts.

"I admire your fortitude, Maude. If it appears you might require counsel, please call upon my husband. He would be honored to serve you."

"What a travesty of justice," Amelia raised her voice, "if Maude were required to appear. She wasn't even a witness to the accident!" Amelia bid two spades.

Looking meaningfully at Margaret, Amelia repeated, "It would be a travesty of justice and in our very own court!"

"Speaking of travesty, have the police caught those hooligans who desecrated your Mercedes with those awful signs in front of Saint Timothy's?"

Maude dabbed at her eyes with a tissue. "No, and I suppose they probably won't bother finding them, either. I tell you being ridiculed and defamed in front of my own church is heart-breaking!"

Maude grabbed another tissue.

"The innocent always suffer the most," Amelia clucked her tongue. "I so admire you, Maude."

"As do all of us," the other two assured her.

Margaret Kenelly eventually won a slam in bridge with Maude's heart support. Margaret left with thanks, repeating pledges of support for Maude from her and her husband. The other two ladies departed soon thereafter.

Maude relaxed in her easy chair and rang for Eunice. "Good work, Eunice, although I thought the salad a bit spicy and the sea bass too dry."

Eunice bowed her head. "I'm sorry, Madame. I'll endeavor to do better in the future."

"And Eunice?"

"Yes, Madame?"

"Bring me a large Bushmills and ice. I feel a small libation is in order to celebrate my planning and preparation of today's successful program."

TWENTY SEVEN

Maude's gloating and reverie was interrupted by Eunice's later announcement. "Father Murphy is here, asking to see you, Madame."

"Oh, my," Maude took a last swallow of the Bushmills and shoved the glass behind the nearest potted plant.

She touched her hair and straightened the skirt. "Show him in."

"Thank you for seeing me, Maude."

"Please have a seat, Father. I confess," she paused, wondering at the appropriateness of her last word, "that I've been intending to come to see you for some time."

"Saint Timothy's is always honored by your presence," he gave a little bow. "We are there to serve your spiritual needs.

"But it's me who's here to confess, Maude. I've come to apologize. In front of the church this morning I found your Mercedes with several signs on it. I think the purpose of the signs is to advertise you as the owner of the car involved in that terrible accident on the N20 the other night.

"I assure you that Saint Timothy's had no part in placing the car or the signs there. I even found a photographer in front of the church, taking pictures of your car. That photograph may mean there's to be another news article in the *Journal*. A story and photo may cause some readers to think Saint Timothy's had a part in this tragedy. I regret that inference very much."

Connor rang the bell at her elbow. "Tea, Father?"

"Only if convenient for you, Maude. I came to apologize

on behalf of our church and to advise you of the possible news coverage. I know your schedule is demanding."

"Father, I thank you for both the unnecessary apology and the warning."

She took a deep breath. "What I wanted to eventually talk to you about is my concern. I think some members of Saint Timothy's are seeking to discredit and humiliate me. A recent example is the vestry's unanimous vote to nominate me as chairperson of the 500th Anniversary celebrations. Obviously, that is a full time responsibility and I'd be effectively excluded from the vestry. I hope that was not your intent."

Murphy accepted a tea. "Thank you, Eunice."

"No, I think it was the vestry's recognition that Saint Timothy's should be represented and that you were our most qualified candidate. I ask for your continued prayers for Saint Timothy's, for its vestry and your priest.

"It's amazing how often the word 'confession' is used today. If you have any desire to seek healing and forgiveness, I assure you I am always available," he studied Maude, hoping she understood.

"At that thought, I must leave. Without invitation, I've taken too much of your valuable time. Are you already involved in your new duties with the Anniversary committees?"

"Yes, Father. We're in the initial stages of organizing the different groups."

"I wish you success," he offered a hand. "Thank you for the excellent tea."

Taking her hand, he looked directly at her. "I pray for you every day, Maude."

She stood at the window for a long time, staring at the priest climb on his old bicycle and slowly pedal away.

Maude considered his words, then remembered the unfinished glass of Bushmills behind the potted plant.

She rang Eunice for more ice.

Inspector O'Bryan was sweating profusely although it was cool in the Superintendent's air-conditioned office. They had been discussing—rather O'Bryan had been interrogated on—his investigation report of the N20 accident.

"Still no identification of the victim?"

"None yet, sir. Our fingerprint section is having trouble reading his prints. Seems they have been partially obliterated."

"Obliterated? How?"

"They think his fingers were sanded, burned or abused in some manner, sir. Makes the prints almost impossible to read. Oftentimes, men in prison do that."

Irritated, Superintendent O'Hagerty stared at the inspector. "Your report is unclear about how the accident happened and who is responsible for failing to lend assistance. to the injured man.

"He's still in the hospital?"

"Yes, sir. Multiple fractures of arms and legs. Plus the usual internal injuries associated with a violent collision. He also suffered a concussion which prevents us getting much information out of him."

"He was clear enough that a black Mercedes hit him!"

"Yes, sir. He was also clear that the Mercedes began to stop, then speeded up and fled the scene. The driver and passenger filed opposite, contradictory statements on the incident."

"What's your assessment of their statements, Inspector?"

"I believe the driver, sir. He swears he was ordered by the passenger not to stop, instead to speed away."

"Yes, I read that. I also saw that ridiculously short statement from the passenger, a Mrs. Connor. She owns that peculiar old structure everyone calls Manor House?"

"Right, sir."

"She's one of the wealthiest ladies in Mallow—maybe the county—and you believe her driver instead?"

O'Hagerty scoffed. "I find it difficult to believe the Director of Public Prosecutions would choose a driver's statement over hers. Why do you believe the driver, what's his name, Summers?"

"That's right. I do, Superintendent."

"Well, spit it out, Inspector. Why?"

"Father Murphy, as you know, is pastor of Saint Timothy's. He assures me that Summers is telling the gospel truth."

O'Hagerty chuckled. "A priest's opinion of 'gospel truth' is hardly admissible in court, Inspector!"

O'Bryan agreed. "I know, Superintendent. That's the problem. The Director of Prosecutions is sure to charge Summers with careless driving and hitting a pedestrian. Withholding assistance is another matter."

The Superintendent heaved a sigh. "Well, I see no alternative to our recommending that Summers be charged for all three offenses. That Connor lady can't be charged on her driver's statement alone.

"Send it over to the DPP."

O'Bryan winced but answered smartly. "Yes, sir."

It made the news! It was the first time that the local papers bore similar morning headlines.

DRIVER CHARGED IN HIT
AND RUN ACCIDENT!

A news release received from the Office of the Director of Public Prosecutions announces that the driver of the vehicle recently striking a pedestrian on the N20 and leaving the scene without offering assistance is being charged with these offenses.

The driver of the automobile, a large Mercedes sedan, is James F. Summers of Riverside, Mallow, remains in police custody.

The male victim of the hit and run, still not positively identified, recuperates in the Mallow Hospital. His injuries include several broken limbs, internal injuries and a concussion inhibiting full memory.

The multiple charges are unexpected due to the driver's assertion, contained in the police report, that he was ordered by his employer not to stop or assist the victim.

In combination, these charges may increase the usual mandatory sentence to imprisonment for a period of twelve months.

Judge F.J. Hanlon, President of the Mallow District Court, will select a solicitor for the defense. A trial date has yet to be determined.

Without a word, Father Murphy passed the front page over the breakfast table to Viola. "I believe Summers, the driver. He told me Maude Connor actually yelled at him not to stop or help the victim lying there on the road."

"You have a kind heart, Father," she resisted the urge to touch his hand.

"What does Maude say?"

"She's noncommittal. But I pray she's examining her conscience. Meanwhile, I'd like to aid Summers's wife and children. He's now unemployed: they need food, money, care…everything."

This time she couldn't resist and patted his hand. "They need uplifting of their spirits, Father. Just like you do for me every single day!"

Frowning with a new thought, he closed his eyes. "Saint Timothy's can't take sides in a criminal case. We can't favor either parishioner."

"Not to worry, Father," she winked. "I'll see to it."

TWENTY EIGHT

As soon as the "good vestry," as they now called themselves, settled at their table in John Long's and ordered drinks, the questions began.

"What's going on, Viola? Something wrong at Saint Timothy's?"

Suspicion spread to others. "Father's not ill or something, is he?"

Viola picked up the bill for their first drink and waved it. "This one's on me," she announced proudly.

She eyed John Reilly, her last questioner. "No, of course not."

"Then why did you call us here?"

Mrs. Kennedy winked at Viola. "Go, ahead. Tell them what you're proposing."

Viola held up the morning newspaper's headline. "Guess you've all seen this about the accident and who's going to trial for it?"

"Who?" chorused Joyce and Pat, who had not.

"The driver of Maude's car, that's Jim Summers, is being charged with the accident…"

"Allow me," interrupted George Bailey, "being charged despite Jim's sworn statement that he was told by 'Her Ladyship' seating in the back seat—naturally—*not* to stop, instead to speed *up*."

"Which she denies," Viola added.

Kennedy broke in with a question. "Who do you think the judge will believe? 'Her Ladyship' or her driver?"

They all answered in unison. "Her Ladyship!"

This time, Viola stood up. "I suggest we do something to prevent this travesty."

"Here, here!" George applauded. "What shall we do? Set fire to her big, black car?"

Viola held up a hand. "I suggest we organize a community march down O'Brien Street to the District Court, supporting Jim Summers. Get the Mallow band and everything!

"Father is concerned about Jim's family now that he's in jail. His wife and two children need money for groceries, heat and light. Let's take up a collection for them during the march to the court.

"Any discussion?"

"Let's do it," cried Mrs. Kennedy. "I'll establish a special account at the bank where we'll deposit the donations."

Not to be outdone, businessman Pat Davis stood. "I'll order an advertisement about the march...let's call it a public, family-friendly parade."

"Day after tomorrow? Starting at 11:00 a.m.? How about starting from here, John Long's, then over to the District Court?"

"Let's do it!"

Once again, Viola held up a small, restraining hand. "Remember this. We are not acting in the name of Saint Timothy's. Our church is not sponsoring this parade nor requesting donations for the Summers family. Understood?"

A chorus of 'Ayes' followed.

Before the "good vestry" went home from John Long's, Joyce MacDoo had written a press release to be given the next morning to the Mallow and Cork newspapers. It detailed the purpose of the parade, times and routes of march, as well as the collection to be made for the benefit of the Summers family.

"How about it, lads?" Joyce handed copies to John Reilly and George Bailey. "I want you to deliver these to the editors of these newspapers and answer any questions. Can do?"

"Sure" John said. "Saint Timothy's is not involved, right?"

"That's right. We don't want Father Murphy or the church involved in Jim's trial. We can't take sides in that fracas."

Mrs. Kennedy was organizing as well. "We meet at my house after dinner tonight and get crackin'. There's lots of work, so we all must pitch in and help.

"You, Joyce, are in charge of making signs to carry in the parade. We'll need lots them. Maybe a hundred!"

"What do the signs say?" Joyce was scribbling in the steno pad she used at the vestry meetings.

"Use your imagination, dear. Things like 'Justice for Jim,' 'Truth Must Prevail.' Ah…how about 'Jim Told the Truth.' I remember from teaching you in elementary school how creative you are."

A pleased Joyce blushed, not looking up from her pad of notes.

"What about me?" Viola nudged Kennedy as she finished with Joyce.

"Viola, I want you to contact the Ladies Social Club, the Red Cross, the Scout Group, and the Archaeological and Historical Society We want them to provide marchers in our parade tomorrow, as many as they can muster. Joyce provides them their signs."

"Now you men," Kennedy paused to catch her breath. "You contact the United Soccer Club and the Carlow to

Cork Tractor Club. Now, the Fire Station is very important. They must give us a fire truck, preferably with a siren, for the parade. Tell them all how important this is to save Jim Summers from twelve months in prison because of 'Her Ladyship's' false statement. There's his poor family to provide for, too. Got that?"

"The 'trio' is on it, Mrs. Kennedy. We'll give it our best." George replied as John and Patrick nodded.

"Oh, that's not all," Kennedy chortled. "Contact that Masonic group in Cork. Masons always like to march in parades with their banners. And the Rotary! Don't forget them, either.

"John," she looked at Reilly, "you must be close with the Farmers' Association."

"You mean the IFA?"

"I do."

"I'll get with 'em right away!"

"But all of you, listen to me. We must stress the parade and collection for the family is not affiliated with Saint Timothy's. We can't support one of our own parishioners and neglect the other because of this trial."

Pat rolled his eyes. "Even if her name is Maude Connor?"

"Even if it's Maude Connor," Kennedy stressed.

"Pat, you're the perfect man to organize the marching groups outside John Long's as they straggle in tomorrow morning. First, organize them in groups, next send them out to march in any order you like. Can you do that?"

"Honored," Pat replied with a little bow. "That will add considerably to my resume when I run for mayor next term."

TWENTY NINE

Mrs. Kennedy watched with delight—almost applauding—as Patrick Davis began the parade with a salute to the fire chief, riding atop Mallow's largest, reddest fire engine. With a blast on the siren, the truck lumbered down O'Brien Street, slow as a circus elephant.

Pat substituted the fire truck ahead of the green-uniformed Irish Farmers' Association brass band. It had been a terse moment with the IFA bandmaster, but Pat easily won, reminding the bandmaster that the truck might be immediately needed in case of a fire somewhere. It should go and finish first, he explained with gestures the equal of any Dublin politician.

"And a fine politician he would be," Kennedy said softly to herself. Momentarily she imagined that Patrick was the ringmaster of a circus, standing in the middle of a vast ring, exhorting the performers in each act to do their best.

"If Pat's a ringmaster, then I'm the puppet master," she lifted her head proudly. After the brass band came members of the United Soccer Club, dressed in their playing uniforms. They'd just interrupted soccer practice to join the parade route to the Court House, which was unexpectedly crowded with spectators.

Between each marching element were carefully placed unofficial members of the Saint Timothy vestry, waving flags and banners being passed out by Joyce MacDoo. 'Rescue His Family' read one huge banner carried between George and Viola. Behind them were more homemade, colorful banners demanding justice for jailed driver Jim Summers.

Not to be outdone by the fire truck were several antique tractors puffing smoke and chugging loudly. John Reilly sat in the seat of one complaining and spitting old tractor, waving his hat and a 'Jim Deserves Justice' flag.

A dozen Masons from Cork wearing their ritual aprons came next, waving 'Truth Must Prevail' posters. Girls and boys in scouting uniforms were next, marching to the beat of a drum being played by a small, sweating but determined young scout.

Kennedy began waving even more fervently as a group representing the Archaeological and Historical Society—most of whom she'd known since childhood—marched by, attempting to keep step with the Scouting Group's drummer.

"What a fine parade...and planned so quickly and executed so well!" Kennedy exclaimed as a group of Rotarians, handing out colored balloons to children along the route, ended the parade. "All we needed was the Mayor and it would have been complete." She looked behind her, wondering if Father Murphy was somewhere in the press of spectators following the marchers to the Court House. She was thankful he was nowhere in sight.

The solicitor appointed to defend Jim Summers, Hiram Fogarty, stood at the top of the Court House steps to welcome the crowd and explain the purpose of the hastily-organized parade. He detailed in a loud voice each charge levied against his client. Between his pauses were 'boos' from the crowd protesting the prosecution's allegations against the driver. Plainly, the crowd favored Jim Summers.

During Fogarty's remarks, Mrs. Kennedy and her

friends circulated among the crowd of spectators carrying black boxes decorated to look like Connor's Mercedes. People were amused by the symbolism and generously filled the little 'cars' with coins and bills for the Summers family.

"Look who's here," Viola nudged Mrs. Kennedy and inclined her head.

Leading a way through the crowd was a burly stranger dressed in chauffer black, clearing a path for the female closely following him.

It was Maude Connor, waving a cheque in the air, attempting to divert the crowd's attention from solicitor Fogarty's appeals for justice for Jim Summers.

Maude's progress through the crowd was captured by a hired photographer, snapping pictures as Maude advanced to the front, still brandishing a bank cheque in the air. The spectators were momentarily distracted from the solicitor's remarks.

"She's going to present it to you," Viola predicted. "A public show of generosity to enhance the crowd's opinion of Maude."

"Plus the judge's, too." Kennedy attempted to smile as Maude closed in.

"Ladies and gentlemen," the chauffer shouted. "Here is Mrs. Maude Connor making a generous gift to the Summers family relief fund."

With a grandiose gesture, Connor presented the cheque to Kennedy. "For the benefit of the family of my driver," she announced as loudly as she could.

The spectators were momentarily quiet, then the gathering began to break up, paraders and spectators going elsewhere.

Elsewhere for the 'good vestry' of Saint Timothy's meant their usual table at John Long's. Congratulating each other on the success of their parade, they grinned, caroused and ordered drinks.

"We should get a discount, Sean!" George Bailey bellowed across the room to the bartender, busily filling pints.

Viola chose a chair next to Kennedy's. "How much did that awful woman donate?"

Kennedy unfolded the cheque and showed it to her. "A thousand euros. Care to bet with me that her photo won't be on page one in the morning's newspaper?"

"No bet. I just hope the parade's mentioned," Viola murmured, distractedly looking around the bar.

Kennedy noted her look but asked anyway. "What's wrong, girl? Worried about the Father?"

Viola bit her lip. "Just a bit. I pray he'll not be in trouble because of the parade."

Suddenly Maude Connor strode up to their table, hands on hips, glaring. "Here you are! All the conspirators gathered together at a bar! What would Father Murphy say?

"Or is he having a slash in the gents' room?"

Mrs. Kennedy stood, eye to eye with Connor and slapped her. "Filthy! How dare you say that about our good Father!"

Maude stepped back, touching her cheek. "He won't be a 'good Father' much longer once I tell the Monsignor and the Bishop about his and your," she eyed the whole table, "interfering and meddling in a criminal trial! I'll see him discredited and out on the street!"

Viola sprung up, next to Maude. "You do something like that and you're sure to come to harm!"

Maude shoved a startled Viola back into her chair. "She just threatened me! Did all of you hear her! Remember what she said! Take me out of this den of vipers!" she ordered her new chauffer.

She glared at each of them sitting around the table. "You're an evil, evil," she struggled for a word, "cabal! You'll all regret your stupid attempts to discredit me!"

John Reilly struggled to his feet and waved at the bartender. "My treat, Sean. All around! We need a celebratory pint or two! Hurrah, she's gone!

"And what about that discount George asked about?"

The crowd in and around the Mallow Court House the next day was so vast that the Superintendent had to borrow a 12-man detail from the Cork Police Station. The spectators who couldn't find standing room in the court room filled all the hallways of the building. The line of waiting, watching people even extended far down O'Brien Street.

"All rise!" the bailiff announced as Judge R.K. Kenelly entered and took his chair at the podium. The customary announcements were made by the bailiff and everyone lucky enough to have a place, sat down.

Judge Kenelly made an unusual and stern announcement himself. "If there are disturbances during this trial, I will order the courtroom cleared. So behave yourselves!"

A large segment of the courtroom had been reserved for reporters representing six national dailies covering this trial, plus their television vans parked outside.

Kenelly removed and polished his glasses. "Proceed."

The public prosecutor stood and read into the record the entirety of the police report of the accident and injury on the N20. Next, he detailed the charges against Summers: negligent driving resulting in serious injury, failing to give aid and assistance, and leaving the scene of a crime. Elements of proof for each charge also were read into the record of trial.

A bewildered and frightened looking Jim Summers sat between two constables. He and his solicitor, Hiram Fogarty, stood and pleaded not guilty to the specified charges.

Lengthy opening statements from prosecution and defense followed. The statements were so long and filled with legalese that many spectators, particularly those queued in O'Brien Street, sought shade, food and drink—especially drink—elsewhere.

Judge Kenelly called for a noon recess but many people occupying good seats in the room preferred staying rather than risk losing their places. At 1:00 p.m. the proceedings resumed and the prosecution called its first witness, Maude Connor.

After being sworn in, she sat down, smiling at Judge Kenelly, whose wife was her frequent bridge partner. She read the short statement given earlier to the police and stopped, looking expectantly at her solicitor.

"No further questions, Your Honor," he quickly responded.

Defense solicitor Fogarty stood and approached Connor to begin his questioning.

"Objection, Your Honor," called Connor's solicitor. "Since the other major witness in this proceeding, the victim of this accident with an automobile, is medically unavailable to be present and to be examined by me, I claim the same right for Mrs. Connor."

The immediate uproar from the spectators prevented even the judge's gavel being heard pounding on the podium. Kenelly looked more angry than perplexed.

Fogarty was on his feet at once. "Objection, Your Honor. I move the words 'accident with an automobile' be stricken from the record and counsel cautioned about such inappropriate language.

"Further, I move the same privilege counsel just claimed for Mrs. Connor be extended to my client. There must be no prosecutorial questions for my client who still suffers, physically and mentally, from this unfortunate but unintended late night accident."

Most of the reporters jumped from their seats to race to the nearest telephone to tell their editors about the apparent impasse and court room melee.

"Objection, Your Honor."

Now it was the counsel's turn. "I move that the words 'unfortunate but unintended late night' be stricken from the record. Counsel well knows such language is unprofessional and misleading."

The enraged judge ordered both counsels to meet him in chambers immediately.

Viola hurried back to the church to tell Father Murphy what happened in the court room. She had persisted that he not attend the trial, especially after the threat made by the enraged Connor in John Long's bar.

She found Murphy kneeling in his usual place near the altar, alternately praying and reading his breviary.

By 4:00 o'clock, the judge and the two solicitors were still closeted in chambers. The court was recessed until 10:00 a.m. the next day.

Two days later, after further explosive day-long court

sessions, Father Murphy sat across the breakfast table with Viola.

Patiently but persistently, she had urged Murphy not to show himself at the courthouse. "Please don't go, Father. Your being there would just add to Maude's malicious claim that you 'meddled and interfered in a criminal case."

Murphy smiled and thanked her for her concern for Saint Timothy's. He picked up and began reading the newspaper's wrap-up account of the entire proceedings, findings and sentencing. Headline-sized photos of both Summers and Connor accompanied the front page article.

DRIVER FOUND GUILTY; RECEIVES MAX SENTENCE FOR ACCIDENT

Mallow District Court Presiding Judge R.K. Kenelly concluded the fractious trial of James Summers, driver of the auto which recently struck and injured a pedestrian along route N20, south of Mallow. Summers was found guilty of all charges and sentenced to twelve months imprisonment.

The trial was long and contentious due to opposing statements from all three witnesses: victim, driver and the driver's employer. According to a statement from the victim, just identified as Joseph Casey, still undergoing treatment and rehabilitation in the Mallow Hospital, he was walking along N20, attempting to catch a ride with passing vehicles. Both the night and his own clothing were dark, he acknowledged. A black vehicle he identified positively as a Mercedes sedan struck him as he motioned for a ride. Although seriously injured, he remembered the Mercedes slowing to stop, he thought, to assist him. Instead the vehicle, later identified as belonging to Mallow resident Mrs. Maude Connor, speeded up and left him seriously injured on the roadway.

The driver of Connor's Mercedes was James Summers, a long time employee of Mrs. Connor. He was returning her to Mallow from a day in Cork. Summers admitted accidentally hitting Casey on the darkened N20 roadway. According to Summers, he was stopping the vehicle in order to assist Casey but his employer, Mrs. Connor in the vehicle's back seat, "yelled at me not to stop, instead, speed up!" He complied with her order, thus leaving the scene without rendering assistance.

Mrs. Connor, a member of one of Mallow's founding families, made a sworn statement that she was asleep in the vehicle's back seat and neither heard nor witnessed any accident. She remained asleep, she maintained, until returned to her Mallow home, Manor House.

Judicial fireworks were created when the Connor's counsel moved that the defense solicitor be prevented from cross-examining the owner of the automobile. The defense solicitor made an identical motion to prelude the counsel from cross-examining the automobile's driver. Both motions were granted by the district judge, setting a highly unusual and controversial legal precedent.

There was an immediate public outcry on hearing the court's findings and punishment of driver Summers, who is married and has two small children. A well-attended parade to the Court House preceded the trial to support Summers's innocence of the 'hit and run' allegation since he was ordered by his employer to *drive away, ignoring the injured Casey. Summers remains in the Mallow jail, pending transfer to Limerick Prison.*

At a public parade preceding the trial a large amount of money was collected by concerned citizens to aid the Summers family during the father's absence.

Citizen protests against the maximum sentencing of Summers continues. A police cordon has been placed around the court house to prevent further damage. Judge R.K. Kennely was unavailable for comment at the time of publication.

THIRTY

Father Murphy jumped up from the table, upsetting his chair

"Viola! Look! The accident victim's name is Casey! Could that be the son she's been so worried about?

"If so, she'll want to go to the hospital immediately to see him. I'd better ring for a taxi to take her there."

Viola stared at the article at which he pointed. "It's a common name but I'll go ask. Don't you think, Father, that I'd better accompany her if she wants to go?"

"Yes, Viola. You're an angel. If you think it alright, I'll go with her to visit him tomorrow."

Resisting the urge to hug the priest, she instead smiled and thanked him for the compliment, as she ran from the room to find Mrs. Casey.

Viola and Mrs. Casey returned to the church later that afternoon. Although still in tears, Casey insisted on thanking Father Murphy for his kindness in sending her to see son, Joe, in the hospital. "Bless you, Father. You're a true Irish saint if ever there was one."

"On with you! I'm not a saint, just another sinner, Mrs. Casey. If you're thanking me for the ride, you're most welcome. How are Joe's injuries healing?"

"The doctor sez he's progressin' slow but sure. Poor lad, he's wrapped up in pulleys and ropes like a captured ape."

Later, Murphy poured and handed Viola a cup of tea despite her blushing protest. "I should be doing that for you, Father."

"Tell me your impressions of Joe."

She thought for a moment. "Lucky he was near a good hospital. Both his arms and both legs are in traction. He also took a good thump to the head. Still, he recognized his mum."

"What do you think of my taking her to see him tomorrow? Or would I be in the way?"

"Go, by all means, Father. Joe may not know you, of course."

"Don't think we've ever met. I don't recall ever seeing him in church with his mother. Have you ever seen him before?"

She put her cup down. "I think so," she thought. "Maybe I've seen him over in the Coffee House a time or two."

Needlessly, he stirred his tea again. "That's interesting," he mused. "Maybe he's…"

Mrs. Casey interrupted, holding the telephone out. "It's for you, Father, that Inspector O'Bryan again."

The next morning Murphy's schedule called for a meeting with the Ladies' Guild.

He and Viola lunched with them at nearby restaurant. On their way back to Saint Timothy's, she touched his sleeve.

"You gave a great little talk on St. Matthew, Father. I had forgotten that he originally was named Levi and was once a despised tax collector."

Murphy nodded thanks, immediately changing the subject. "Time for Mrs. Casey and I to get out to the hospital and check on Joe. Want to go with us?"

"Thanks, but I'd better stay here and answer the

telephone. Maybe Maude Connor will call and invite us for a lavish dinner at Manor House."

"Ah, the power of prayer," Murphy quipped as he held the taxi door for Mrs. Casey.

"Did you follow the trial closely, Father?" Casey asked as they settled into the taxi.

"No, I didn't. Viola thought I shouldn't attend because Mrs. Connor recently accused me of interfering with the case."

"Ah, a terrible woman! Don't you agree, Father?"

Murphy squirmed, seeking a pastoral response. "Judge not, that you be not judged," he quoted the well-known verse from Matthew that he'd used at the ladies' luncheon.

To his surprise, Casey immediately responded with "For with the judgment you pronounce, you will be judged."

"That's very good, Mrs. Casey. I'm impressed."

Once inside Joe's room at the Mallow Hospital. Murphy caught his breath, seeing the severity of the young man's injuries. "Are you receiving good care, Joe?"

"Yes, Father, it's class. Thank you for bringing my mother."

At this, Mrs. Casey handed Joe a box of candies. "My boy always loved his sweets," she beamed.

Murphy took from his coat the gift Viola had provided him. It was a short history of the Irish national football team. "Maybe this will occupy a little time once you have full use of your hands, Joe."

After an hour of visiting, a nurse entered and handed Joe several pills. "These will make you a bit groggy," she explained to the visitors as well as her patient. To them, she turned. "He needs to rest now."

On the way back to Saint Timothy's, Mrs. Casey asked "Do you believe that driver or Mrs. Connor, Father?"

"You mean about the…"

"About Mrs. Connor telling the driver to go on and not bother with my son lying there broken and bleeding on the pavement?"

Murphy sighed, facing her. "I don't know all the facts about the accident, Mrs. Casey, but I tend to believe Jim, the driver."

"Why do you believe him instead of Maude Connor?"

Hesitating, he shrugged. "Because of the seal, I cannot answer your question."

She leaned forward as the taxi stopped in front of Saint Timothy's. "The seal of the confessional?"

He only nodded in response.

"Don't you wish you could get Maude into that confessional, Father?"

His answer was a half-smile and shrug.

National news quickly became dull due to its concentration on continuing economic difficulties with the European Union and the euro. Once the public outcry about the results of a hit and run trial in Mallow reached Dublin, several radio and television stations dispatched teams to the town. One of them, RTE News, immediately covered the furor, blanketing the town overnight with television and radio.

Two television vans stationed in front of the Court House attracted many of the original protesters, still angry, to return to the scene. Summers's defense solicitor, Mr. Fogarty, instantly appeared on several newscasts, shaking either his head or his fists in frustration in the best courtroom manner.

"My client has been denied a fundamental right, that of cross examination of a hostile witness. Mrs. Connor's short, written statement that she was asleep and saw no accident demands clarification. Of itself, without examination, her statement is suspect. I am raising this travesty of justice with the President of the District Court, His Honor Judge F.J. Hanlon. Lacking satisfaction, I intend to communicate with the High Court in Dublin for remedy."

"Presiding at the Mallow District Court, Judge R.K. Kenelly declined comment," added the interviewer.

"Turn on the telly!" Mrs. Casey gestured. "There's big news about Joe's trial!"

Father Murphy flicked-on the black and white TV on the small dining table where he sat, reviewing the budget. Mrs. Casey pulled up a chair, soon followed by Viola from her office.

Transfixed, the three watched the story appearing all over Ireland at that moment about Mallow's trial and public protest.

"Joe's famous!" Casey intoned.

Murphy and Viola looked at each other. "Hopefully, not *infamous*."

Viola nodded agreement at their assessment.

At the Manor House, Maude Connor's scream was heard throughout the mansion. Eunice, the housekeeper, came running to the parlor where Connor stood, gesturing at the large color television set.

"My God!" Connor cried. "They're talking about the trial! Now I'll be mocked over all Ireland! I won't be able to go shopping or to the theatre…or anywhere!"

She flopped down on the divan and hooked her finger at Eunice. "Bushmills and ice. A big one!"

After consuming the drink, Maude sat with the telephone in her lap.

She signaled Eunice for another glass, murmuring to herself.

"First, I'll call my solicitor to come here.

"No, first I'd better ask Father Murphy instead.

"No, I can't do that after I told Viola I'm complaining to the Monsignor and the Bishop about him.

"What's first priority? I need the solicitor to start my action against that Fogarty person and all those TV stations. All of them!"

"Thank you for coming so quickly, Father." He was met at the door of Connor's home by a worried Eunice.

"She's ill?"

"Yes, Father." Eunice illustrated by touching a finger to her head. "I think it's mostly nervousness and tension but you'd better ask the doctor. He's in there now."

"Thanks. I'll wait for him." Murphy took a seat, nodding at James H. Polk, the well known, expensive solicitor occasionally employed by Connor.

"I've seen her already," Polk smiled. "Seems quite lucid to me. She's eager to bring defamation charges against that quack solicitor, Fogarty, and all of the radio and TV stations carrying his insidious remarks."

Stepping out of Maude's bedroom, Doctor Hogan overheard Polk's words.

"The defamation charges you speak of," the doctor

stepped up to Polk, "appear to me to be the real cause of her condition. You've upset her by encouraging more law suites.

"You'd do Mrs. Connor, and me—her physician—a great favor by not speaking to her about them at least for several days."

The doctor turned to Murphy. "Were you also summoned, Father?"

"Yes, Eunice called me to come. If Mrs. Connor's alright now, I'll leave unless she wants to see me."

Doctor Hogan held up a restraining hand. "For all of you, I've just given Mrs. Connor a sedative to calm her down. She's in no condition to sign documents, make important decisions—things of that sort—for at least 24 hours. Understood?"

Eunice and the two men nodded in unison.

"Madame does want to see you, Father," Eunice injected. "She told me so, just as Mr. Polk left her."

Eunice opened the bedroom door and gestured.

"If you gentlemen will excuse me," Murphy walked through the door and closed it behind him.

Maude Connor sat upright in the midst of a large, silken bed.

"Sorry you aren't feeling well, Maude," he began, pulling a chair closer to her bed.

"How may I help you?"

Even prone in bed, Maude Connor looked in full control, as if she were a corporate CEO at the head of the conference table. "What I'd like from you, Father, is an honest opinion."

"Certainly. What about?"

"I'm initiating legal suites against several organizations

177

and that Fogarty, the defense solicitor who publicly demeaned me on television. You saw it?"

"Yes, Maude." He reached for his pen. "I know that was very upsetting for you."

"In your opinion," she touched her just-coiffed hair, "will my suites be successful?"

Murphy leaned forward, uncertain he understood. "I can only advise you on matters of the soul, Maude, not law. I just heard Doctor Hogan say that those proposed suites may be the reason you're not feeling well."

"Not feeling well, indeed! How dare he reveal my condition to others! That's not professional!"

"I'm certain Doctor Hogan has your well being in mind, just as I do. I'm concerned with your soul, Maude, not earthly concerns like these legal actions you envision."

She shut her eyes and made fists at his response.

"Would you like communion?"

Opening her eyes, she glared at him. "No, Father. I'm capable, as always, of making my own decisions. And communions can wait until Sundays.

"Or," she stiffened, "are you going to deny me the sacraments just as you allowed your vestry to oust me?"

He hesitated. "A horrible question! I would never deny you the sacraments. Maude. Apparently I've offended you and for that I'm heartily sorry. I'm overjoyed that you're considering communion.

"If not communion here, would you prefer confession?"

"I'm not ready for that, Father. I still have my wits about me, thank you."

"Maude, can we, at least, say a prayer together?"

Without waiting for her answer, he knelt beside the bed and crossed himself.

"Oh, God, let me not lose faith in other people,

"Keep me sweet and sound of heart, in spite of treachery, ingratitude or meanness,"

He paused, listening if she was repeating the words. She did not, but he continued, hoping she would.

"Open wide the eyes of my soul that I may see good in all things,

"And inspire me with the spirit of joy and gladness, in the name of our Lord and Savior. Amen."

Connor finally spoke. "I know what you're trying to convince me to do, Father. I'm not ready."

"Call me whenever I can help, Maude. I am always ready."

With that, he blessed her and departed.

THIRTY ONE

"Oh, Father! You've ripped the seam of your trousers!" Mrs. Casey pointed at one priestly trouser leg.

"Sorry." Bicycling home, while revisiting the conversation with Connor, he'd caught a trouser in the bike sprocket.

"Get them off, Father, and I'll patch them right away. They're your best pair," she admonished, turning her back on him once they were in his office.

Rather than argue, he submitted, handing the torn garment over her shoulder.

"Know where Viola might be?" he asked. "I need to see or speak to her right away."

Mrs. Casey still had her back to Murphy, standing there minus trousers. "Perhaps she should telephone you rather than visit at this moment, Father."

Casey suppressed a giggle. "That is, until I get these mended and back on you."

Realizing his lack of trousers precluded Viola's visit, Murphy agreed. "Thank you, Mrs. Casey. Will you be long sewing them up?"

Waiting on his trousers gave Murphy time to reflect on the three parishioners of Saint Timothy's for whom he sought relief. There was Maude Connor, who probably lied to the police about her part in the auto accident.

John Summers, her driver, soon would be on his way to prison for twelve months, convicted for causing an accident and leaving the scene without assisting the victim.

Accident victim, Joe Casey, son of his housekeeper, was

still hospitalized for serious injuries. Joe's recollections of the accident substantiated Summers's claim that he attempted to stop and assist Joe.

Murphy hid his face in his hands. What are my responsibilities to each of these? His thoughts were curtailed by the telephone. It was Viola.

"Father, are you alright? Mrs. Casey said you want to see me but that I can't come immediately."

"I'm fine, Viola, just waiting for my trousers to be repaired. What I'd like you to do for me is schedule a meeting of the vestry this evening after services. I want the meeting to be held in the chapel, rather in the parlor where we usually gather."

"May I ask why there, Father?"

"I plan on giving a short homily on forgiveness and think that's the ideal place for my subject."

"After services? Alright, Father. Meanwhile, when may I come to see you about next week's schedule?"

He grimaced. "Not until I'm fully clothed. I'll let you know."

Her response was a muffled giggle.

Three vestry members—George, John and Pat—were the first to arrive in the chapel for the vestry meeting. "Why here?" they wondered as they sat down.

"We've done something serious," whispered John Reilly.

"Right," Pat muttered. "Father's going to read the riot act to us about something. Maybe the black Mercedes we parked in front of the church."

"No, it's about our parade," whispered George.

Pat retorted. "Not *our* parade. It was a concerned citizens' parade."

By then the female members of the vestry were seated alongside the male trio. Joyce was the first to enter the pew, followed by Viola. To ease her entry, they left the next-to-the aisle space vacant for Mrs. Kennedy, who limped in, last.

They all stood as Father Murphy entered the chapel from the rear. He immediately motioned for them to sit down. "Thank you for coming on short notice. The fault was mine, not Viola's, as usual.

"I chose the chapel as our unusual meeting place today. I did so because to me just being here instills a sense of peace uncommon elsewhere."

With that, Murphy led them in a short opening prayer, ending with "Open wide the eyes of my soul that I may see good in all things."

"Since we are representative of our entire congregation, I thought it useful for us to gather here to reflect and pray for four members of Saint Timothy's.

"First is Maude Connor, downcast that we have excluded her from the vestry, unnerved by the accident on N20 and contemplating legal actions against those she claims defamed her publicly. As a result, Maude is under a doctor's care at home.

"I ask your prayer and intercession for this troubled lady whom we all know."

There followed a long period of silent prayer, after which Murphy resumed.

"The second individual, known to most of us, is John Summers, Maude's driver. He has been convicted of causing the accident and leaving without assisting the seriously injured individual he hit. John is on the way to prison for twelve months, leaving his family of wife and two small children, bereft.

"Please pray for the welfare of John's family. Pray for relief from the sentence meted John, perhaps unjustly."

Another period of silence and prayer followed.

"I know from the newspaper that a group of generous people, perhaps including some of you, collected funds for John's family. We owe those unknown individuals our thanks for both their concern and assistance.

"The third person for whom I ask your prayers is the victim of that accident. He is Joe, son of Mrs. Casey, our housekeeper. Pray that Joe's pain may be eased, that his injuries healed and that he find employment once released.

"I ask your prayers also for a fourth person, Mrs. Casey, that she may harbor no resentment against Maude Connor who may have delayed medical treatment for Joe."

With that, Murphy said a closing prayer and thanked them again for attending.

Later Viola knocked on his office door and entered. She had been crying and Murphy stood and hurried forward. "What's wrong?"

"I want to tell you how affected most of us were by your words, Father. I think you caused us all to examine our consciences. You certainly did me.

"I ask forgiveness for impure thoughts," she blushed, adding quickly "about Maude."

"Do you desire confession?"

"Yes, Father."

They knelt on the office floor and softly began the sacrament.

THIRTY TWO

"Hey, Sean! Three pints over here!" The males of the 'best vestry' were ready for a drink following their unusual meeting with their priest in the chapel.

George Bailey pounded on their table with a fist. "Jesus, I feel like I'm the devil's disciple after what Father said."

John Reilly was shocked and immediately warned, "Hush, you don't mean that George!"

"You mean you enjoyed that session with the Father?"

Pat Davis sat in the corner, enjoying their banter. "Father was doing the right thing," he said, "getting us all back on the straight and narrow, so to speak."

George put down his pint to look at his chums. "There was a secret message in the Father's talk, wasn't there?"

"Go on with you!" John raised his glass. "Here's to Father Murphy, bless his soul for trying to uplift us heathens!"

"What was the message?"

Pat came alive in the corner. "His message is that one of those people he told us about is a devil and needs eliminating."

"Explain that," demanded George.

Pat signaled for another round before beginning. "First, that accident alerts us to our biggest problem in Mallow. Answer this question. Did Summers stop to give poor injured Joey assistance or not?"

"Summers said he was told by Maude to keep going, not even to slow down."

"And according to Maude," Pat added, grinning, "the grand lady was asleep in the back of her expensive German car and didn't see or hear anything until she was safely deposited by her faithful driver at her luxurious mansion."

"If Maude lied about the accident, it means Summers really did try to stop. He was sentenced for something he didn't do. Maude was the perpetrator of this whole mess and ought to be charged with lying in court, at the very least."

"If she lied," John reasoned, "the driver's sentence is unjust."

Pat leaned back against the wall, staring at his companions. "Then we've uncovered the devil in our midst, lads. What are we going to do about it?"

The three sat back, for a long period, uncomfortable with Pat's question.

Finally, George spoke. "I've got an idea. If we do it right, Mallow is rid of that devil. No one will know we had anything to do with it."

Mrs. Casey knocked on his door. "Come in," he smiled, seeing her peek inside. "You needn't be so formal, Mrs. Casey. What may I do for you? How's Joe getting along? Perhaps we might visit him this afternoon?"

Shivering, she crossed herself. "Oh, Father, thank you."

Since the gesture was unusual for her except during services, Murphy stood up, startled.

"There's a strange man here wanting to see you, Father."

"Did he do something to disturb you?"

"No, Father. But he looked at me queerly and he's carrying a large box."

Murphy sat down. "Know his name?"

"No, Father. Says he's been here before. He's from Kinsale."

"Ah, it must be that Mr. Evers from that Temple of

the Augury group over there. Please show him in and have yourself a good hot scald and a bit of a rest. You look weary."

Carrying a large mailing box, Timothy Evers stepped into the office with a pensive look. As before, his clothing was totally black but fashionable. "You remember me, Father?"

"Of course, Mr. Evers. Have a seat, please, and set your burden down. How are things at the temple?"

Evers gazed at the office ceiling for a moment. "Quite well, thank you. I've come to inquire about you and your church here. Secondarily, I wanted to personally return these valuable articles which I believe were stolen from Saint Timothy's."

Murphy shook hands, next opened the box which Evers had set on the desk.

"Praise the Lord!" Murphy blurted, holding aloft an item from the box. It was a large silver platen.

Astonished, he looked at Evers. "Where did you get these?" Next he extracted a pair of silver chalice.

Evers sat heavily. "Our Temple van was stolen several weeks ago. I reported it to the police and they returned the vehicle to me yesterday. The young girl driving our van was apprehended by the police at a border crossing with Northern Ireland near Clones. Four old, probably very valuable, silver items were found in the van. They matched the police description of articles taken from Saint Timothy's.

"Are they yours, Father?"

"Mr. Evers," Murphy began pumping the other's hand, "I cannot adequately speak—much less thank you—but I'm trying.

"Thank you! These platen and chalice have been a

part of Saint Timothy's since its founding. Thank you for returning them."

"You're welcome, Father. My primary reason for this visit—to advise you of another vision—may not be as welcome as the silver ware."

"Sir, you and your congregation are always welcome at Saint Timothy's!" Murphy sat down, replacing the silver pieces in the box and packing his pipe. "I take it you've had further ...err...how did you put it? *Premonitions* about Saint Timothy's?"

"Visions, Father, visions. Yes, that's also why I'm here, to recount for you my latest vision."

Evers rubbed his forehead. "I hope that you will take precautions so that these visions are blocked and cannot become reality.

"Could we visit your chapel? That's the location of my latest vision. Were I to actually see it, perhaps the dream is applicable elsewhere and I'm simply confused, having been here before."

"Certainly, Mr. Evers. Would you care for a cup of tea before seeing the chapel?"

"Thank you, no. If my vision is errant, I must hurry to find its real location and attempt to prevent the terrible events I envisioned."

They walked quickly to the chapel, going through the sacristy with its hanging robes and vestments. Evers walked slowly, moving his eyes slowly from side to side as if seeking a specific spot in the chapel.

"It *was* here, in this chapel," Evers whispered, stopping.

"I saw blazes enveloping and burning something over

there." He pointed toward the west wall. Suddenly he moved to the nearest pew, sat and held his head as if ill.

"Are you alright?" Murphy hovered over him. "May I get you a glass of water?"

Face drawn, Evers looked up. "No, thank you," he gulped. "This is definitely the place where I saw not only fire. Also I saw death here!

"You must believe me, Father! You must immediately take precautions to prevent fire and death here in your chapel.

"This is the second time I've witnessed these evil events! They must happen unless you prevent them!

"Please help me to my car. I'm exhausted. I must get out of here and back to my temple for cleansing."

More than ever concerned about Evers' health, Murphy took his visitor by the arm and helped him out of the chapel. Outside, in sunshine and fresh air, Evers seemed partially revived.

"Are you certain you are able to drive safely, Mr. Evers? Please allow me to call a doctor to examine you before you leave."

"No, no, Father. My purpose here is fulfilled. I have alerted you to what may happen soon in Saint Timothy's. My thoughts for your safety are with you and your church. I must return to the temple."

Murphy stood on the kerb, watching the SUV drive away. He waved a hand but none was returned.

Inside, he called for Viola. "Come here a moment. Look what has been restored to Saint Timothy's!

"Mrs. Casey, bring us all tea, please. We're celebrating the return of our stolen silver!"

To himself, Murphy added, "I'd better call Inspector O'Bryan and tell him the good news, too."

Slowly pedaling his 'High Nelly' bike, Murphy made it to the police station and asked to see Inspector O'Bryan.

The duty sergeant looked doubtfully at the priest juggling papers in one hand and standing-up a bicycle with the other. "Is he expecting you, Father?"

"No, I don't have an appointment."

"Who's out there? Fergus?" O'Bryan called from inside his office.

"Father Murphy," Murphy provided his name.

"Father Murphy, sir," the sergeant repeated loudly.

"Well, send him in, man. Send him in."

"Thanks for seeing me, as unexpected as always," Murphy bantered.

"Coffee or tea, Father?"

"Delighted, if yourself are having a cup, Inspector."

As cups and biscuits were being carried in and distributed, Murphy began. "I have a very big request to make concerning that Joe Casey, still hospitalized as you know.

"I'm guessing you also know, Inspector, that Joe was the male member of the two thieves attempting to rob the Coffee House last month."

Anxious to add his own information, O'Bryan added. "Yes, Father. The Monaghan police caught the female suspect the other day and returned her to prison awaiting trial for auto theft. The stolen vehicle was returned, as was the silverware stolen from Saint Timothy's. True?"

"All true, Inspector. I thank you and the force mightily

for the return of our cherished old silver. As I said, I've also come asking for a large favor about young Joe."

"No promises, Father, but try me."

"My interest in that troubled young man is because he is—or was—a communicant of Saint Timothy's. His mother even works for Saint Timothy's as our housekeeper. I'm asking your consideration of releasing Joe to Saint Timothy's after his recovery and rehabilitation, based on the following."

Murphy began presenting papers, one at a time. "This is Doctor Connelly's statement that Joe suffers from a concussion with probable long-term consequences. His memory loss is extensive and may be permanent."

O'Bryan was nodding. "We already know that, Father."

Murphy continued. "This paper is from the owner of the Coffee House. He agrees to withdraw his charges if Joe works in his establishment for a period of three months to replace the glassware and other items destroyed during that abortive robbery.

"This next paper is my promise to provide Joe a place to live at Saint Timothy's for a period of one year if he is not prosecuted for the Coffee House illegal entry and attempted robbery."

"Good Lord!" O'Bryan looked heavenward.

"Excuse me, Father," he caught himself. "Is that all you want? How about granting him a police pension for life as well?"

Smiling, Murphy held up a finger. "Excuse *me,* Inspector. I forgot to add that Joe will be under his mother's strict supervision while living with us at Saint Timothy's.

"Please discuss my proposal with the Superintendent

and the Director of Public Prosecutions. If this succeeds, you will have rehabilitated a young man's failed life."

"We'll consider it," O'Bryan stood. "Next time, the coffee's on you, Father."

With that, he firmly escorted Murphy to the station door.

THIRTY THREE

On his return to the church, Murphy found Viola and Mrs. Casey polishing the recovered silver in the parlor. "If I may interrupt you ladies a moment? I need to mention plans for our future.

"As you know, I've been at the police, talking to Inspector O'Bryan about Joe," he eyed Mrs. Casey.

"What I'm trying to do is—once he's well—get his prosecution for the Coffee House break-in suspended. He could live here with us and work at the Coffee House repaying for the items broken during the attempted theft. After that, he can find a permanent job of his liking."

"Bless you, Father!" Mrs. Casey was on her feet and about to hug Murphy but caught herself. "Thank you, thank you, Father! You're a saint!"

"No, I'm certainly not! Let's pray that the police and Public Prosecutor will relent and suspend that prosecution."

Viola clapped her hands excitedly. "She's right! You are a saint, Father. What a blessing to be here, working for you at Saint Timothy's!"

Murphy grinned but tried to calm the two. "It's just a plan I thought to share with you. Speaking of plans, here's another one I should mention.

"Remember the Bishop's surprise visit last week? He wants us to develop a method of training newly-ordained priests here at Saint Timothy's about how to—I'll call it—nurture their parishioners. I mean topics like encouraging the mothers' league, the altar guild, the kindergarten, watching the budget, delegating chores to the vestry, the selection of youth counselors. Get the idea?"

They both nodded.

"I'll need your help on ideas how to accomplish this. I presume we'd be assigned a priest fresh out of seminary, bring him here to live with us and give him on-the-job training how to care for his first congregation. Those are examples which most seminaries don't even mention."

Excitement gone, Viola held up a hand. "Does that mean we—Saint Timothy's—would lose you to another church?"

He paused, not expecting the question. Their smiles dimmed as he frowned before answering. "No, I don't think so. We—you and I—will be here, advising and training new priests until the Bishop thinks otherwise."

He resisted the urge to nudge Viola. "You're not getting rid of old Aloysis T. Murphy as easily as that!"

That afternoon Viola answered the telephone and transferred the call to his office. "Father Murphy here.

"Yes, Maude, are you feeling better?" he answered. "Certainly, you're always welcome! I plan to be here all afternoon. What time is convenient for you?"

Maude Connor arrived at the agreed hour and sat, sipping tea, in Murphy's office.

She looked around the room furtively. "Can we be overheard here, Father?"

He got up and closed the open door. "No, Maude. No one can hear us."

She seemed to relax and extracted a cigarette from a large purse. "Join me, Father?"

He leaned forward to light her cigarette. "No, but may I smoke my pipe?"

At her nod, Murphy packed his pipe and lit it. "Are you needing the sacrament of penance?"

"Is that the same as confession, Father?"

"It is."

"You know, I've been a member of Saint Timothy's for many years, yet have lots of questions about confession."

"Then, let's attempt to answer them here," he suggested, setting aside the pipe.

Maude finished the cigarette and crushed it out in a tray. "I haven't been to confession in so long that I need a refresher course. How often should I go?"

"The norm is every month or every week. Frequency isn't as important as our intent to cleanse ourselves of sin and attempt to sin no more.

"The spiritual basis for confession comes from several sources, among them, James 5:16. 'Confess therefore your sins one to another, and pray one for another, that you may be saved.'"

Distraught, Maude covered her face with both hands. "I'm afraid, Father. I'm terribly afraid," she whimpered.

Without looking up, she added. "I may seem to be proud and virtuous but I fear the hereafter."

Murphy patted her hand. "None of us are without failings, Maude, me especially," and handed her a tissue from the desk.

"I suggest you pray about what you consider your failings. After serious consideration of what you've done or left undone, confession is the next step for your healing and peace of mind."

"How does one confess? I haven't done it in so long, I've forgotten, Father."

"It's not difficult, Maude. I can hear your confession here and now or in the church or anywhere else of your choosing, and at the time of your choosing. But don't delay too long."

"Oh, no, Father. I'm not ready yet," she wiped her nose with another tissue. "Could I see where confessions are held inside the chapel?

"If I decide to do it, I want it done the proper and formal way, with nothing left to chance."

"If your intentions to lead a new life are genuine, there's no chance involved, no matter the setting. Of course, I'll show you the confessional in our chapel if you like. You've seen it thousands of times but not, I think, with the clarity of intent I detect now."

With that, he led her straight to the chapel. "Shall we first have a short prayer? Then we'll examine the confessional if you like."

They knelt, each repeating private prayers. When finished, Murphy rose and blessed her, then pointed to the old confessional box.

"As you probably remember, our confessional box is ancient. It's been here since Saint Timothy's founding in which your family took part."

She moved her hand slowly over the polished finish of the box. "I remember this little door from my earliest years. Going inside and shutting out the world always took my breath away."

Smiling at her memories, she later followed Murphy

outside into the bright sunlight. "I'll give serious thought to your words, Father. I'll contact you when I'm ready…"

"Another thing, Father," her voice cracked. "What I say in confession is absolutely secret, right? A priest cannot divulge anything said in confession. Am I correct?"

"Absolutely," he assured her. "Not even if you told me you'd just shot the President of Ireland."

Parked in front of the church was the black Mercedes with the new driver standing beside her door. Watching the car leave, Murphy stood for a long time, thinking of what Connor had said and how he might help on her return.

"Mrs. Kennedy wants to speak to you, Viola," Mrs. Casey held out her cell phone.

"Good morning, Mrs. Kennedy. This is Viola. How are you?"

"Leery, I think is the word, dear. Leery."

"Why so?"

Mrs. Kennedy looked absently at her diamond ring as she arranged her thoughts. "I heard that Maude came to the Father for counseling. That can't be good. That's like a tiger trading its stripes for a loin cloth."

"You have very good intelligence. It's true she was here for some time in his office, afterwards they walked into the chapel. What they did there, I don't know."

"You should know, dear. She's dangerous. Did you forget she wants you and the Father transferred to the Aran Islands?"

"I'll ask Amos and Mrs. Casey. One of them is certain to know what they were doing in there."

"Thanks, dear. Whatever it was, I bet Maude was not

just there to pray. Let me know, please? I'm afraid she's starting a new campaign against Saint Timothy's."

Later, Viola was able to respond to Kennedy's question. "Mrs. Casey told me they looked at that old confessional on the west side. Apparently Maude's considering confessing her sins. Another win for our saintly priest!"

Mrs. Kennedy admired her diamonds again. "Pray that fine man may not be eaten alive by that scrappy old tiger! Keep both eyes on her, please. I'm more concerned than ever."

Outside, on the west side of the church, George, Pat and John were discussing their new voluntary chore to improve the church's appearance.

Pat picked up a long handled spade. "Seems to me the vestry ladies would be better than us about selecting the best ornamentals to be planted out here."

George demurred. "At least they gave us a choice. We could be dusting and cleaning those chapel rafters, instead. Heights make me dizzy."

Usually taciturn John Reilly nodded, selected a pick and spit on his palms. "Where do we plant them?"

"Depends which variety we choose to plant, John. Some ornamentals grow as big as rowans."

"Now there's a fine tree," Pat lit a cigarette while pointing out prospective digging sites. "Red and yellow foliage in autumn, next, sprays of white flowers followed by those little red berries. But, of course a rowan would grow upward, taller than our spire here."

"Mrs. Kennedy, gents," George reminded, "wants them

to be colorful and short so's not to hide the stained glass windows on this side of the church."

"I say, let's plant yews. The yew only grows to about three meters," Pat illustrated by holding up a hand, "and it looks like a real tree, not a pussy willow or something."

"Why didn't Mrs. Kennedy just tell us unpaid, unskilled laborers which tree to plant?"

"She's too busy worrying about what new antics Maude has in mind to replace us with zombies on the vestry. What about you, John?"

"Well now," he rubbed his big hands together. "I favor the little tree the missus made me plant at home. The Kilmarnock willow, it's called. Fairly short it is and sports pretty grey and yellow catkins."

"Yeah, I know that tree," Pat stamped out his cigarette. "Tha's a good choice, John. I go for it. How about you, George?"

George took off his jacket, folded and laid it carefully on the ground. "Let's go ahead and dig those holes while we have shovels and pick handy."

Amos, the church sexton, ambled up as the three began selecting planting places for the eventual willows. "Congratulations, gents. I see us 'Shanty Irish' as her ladyship calls us are hard at work. Think her day of reckoning will come afore you plant them willows?"

Viola and Mrs. Casey sat at the dining table sipping tea and nibbling the hot scones that Viola had just taken out of the oven.

"Delicious, Viola," Casey smacked her lips in

appreciation. "You'll make some man a fine wife and cook. Have anyone in mind?"

"Glad you like the scones," Viola hesitated, knowing she was being teased. Mrs. Casey knew full well of Viola's affection for Father Murphy.

"No one in particular. I'm still searching for that perfect man." To hide her blush, Viola refilled their cups.

"Where is that man?" Casey asked mischievously.

"The Father?"

"Isn't he *that* man?"

"Father is off visiting that orphanage in Woodbridge."

Casey patted Viola's hand. "I saw the Father the other day, pedaling that old bicycle of his down toward the town centre. The wind was so strong it almost blew him into the river. He's too frail and needs fattening up by a good wife and cook."

Viola grinned at the thought. "If you'll allow me the use of the kitchen tomorrow evening…"

"Of course."

"I'll cook my mother's recipe for lamb stew for us all. We'll get some food into that man."

"A good man, isn't he, dear?"

"The best!"

Casey patted Viola's hand again. "Wonder if he is good enough to forgive Maude Connor's many sins?

"Do you know," she continued, face reddening, "what would have happened had that ambulance been any later in getting my Joe to the hospital?"

Still thinking about cooking for Murphy, Viola shook her head.

"They would have taken his broken body to the morgue

instead of to the hospital! That terribly wicked woman ignored Joe—bloody and unconscious as he was—after her car knocked him down. Why, she even ordered the poor driver to speed up and take her back to that mansion. I'd like to see her so-called 'Manor House' burn to the ground!"

Casey took a deep breath and crossed herself before adding, "And may that one burn in hell!"

Viola was shocked. As soon as she could speak, she scolded. "I know you don't really mean that. Father always says that we must make allowances for others. Hate their sin but love them nonetheless."

"Father hasn't a son, dear. If he did, he'd feel the same way as me. That man is too innocent, too forgiving, too generous."

Viola slammed down her cup, almost chipping it. "You're right! You and I must protect Father from that conniving witch. Let's pledge, you and I, right here."

"To do what?"

"Protect Father Murphy from her in every way possible."

Casey studied Viola "What if that way is illegal?"

Viola didn't blink. "Every way possible," she repeated.

THIRTY FOUR

Early the next morning, Maude Connor was again on the telephone for Father Murphy. "I couldn't sleep last night, Father. I want to come and make my confession right now and in the chapel."

"Certainly, Maude. May God bless your intention. Shall I meet you in my office?"

"Oh, no, Father. If I come to your office, I'll lose what courage I have. I want to meet you at the confessional in thirty minutes."

"I'll be there, Maude. I'm pleased you have made this decision to assure where you'll spend eternity. Thirty minutes," he repeated.

Murphy stood, brushed off his best hassock and prepared to go early to the chapel to meet her. He stepped out of the office just as Viola hurried up, looking unusually anxious.

"Father, the Bishop just arrived out front and wants to meet you in your office immediately."

Murphy checked his watch. "If I'm still with the Bishop in thirty minutes—which is likely—will you please go to the chapel and tell Maude I'm unexpectedly delayed by the Bishop's surprise arrival? I'll be there for her confession as soon as possible.

"Sorry to ask you to do this, Viola," he apologized. "But it's very important that Maude get that message. She may be inside the confessional already, rather than sitting beside it."

"Don't worry, Father. I'll tell her right away."

Under her breath, she added as she hurried to the chapel, "Don't you know yet? I'd do anything for you."

The Bishop's arrival in his big sedan caused a slight sensation in the whole neighborhood. George, Pat and John were digging outside the church as was Amos, the sexton.

As Viola left, she told Mrs. Casey about her chore for Father Murphy. In the chapel she found Maude Connor and explained the probable delay. She returned to her desk and dutifully telephoned Mrs. Kennedy with the unusual news that both the Bishop and Maude were at Saint Timothy's.

"An interesting morning, eh?" Kennedy seemed her usual calm, appraising self. "I wonder if the presence of both of them is part of a plan? Maybe Maude's undertaking some new idea to get Father Murphy reassigned."

Viola protested. "But the Bishop told us in that vestry meeting when he was last here, that he wouldn't…"

Kennedy interrupted. "Haruump! That woman may have changed the Bishop's mind a hundred times since then. I'm coming there right this minute to see what's going on. Keep an eye on Maude for me."

Inside the office with the Bishop seated comfortably, Viola offered tea to the two men. "Mrs. Casey has a delightful Lapsang she's been anxious to serve."

"Thank you, Viola," the Bishop smiled. "I'm just here for a quick visit, then on to another meeting in Fermoy," he frowned at his watch, "for which I'm already late."

"Sorry, Father," he turned to Murphy. "Seems like I use Saint Timothy's as a way station, doesn't it? That's not my intent as I know this is a strong spiritual bastion in our diocese."

"Your visits are always welcome, Excellency. We are honored by them, however short."

The Bishop tapped a folder he'd brought with him.

"I've gone over your outline of training ideas for our newly-ordained priests. It's a grand start, Father. Do you think your proposal could apply to more than one priest at a time?"

Murphy paused, knowing he must choose his words carefully. "Excellency, I think that's possible but it would lengthen the time each individual would have to spend at Saint Timothy's. From my experience, the new priest is so anxious to get to his first assignment that any longer training might prove counterproductive.

"Perhaps, Saint Michael's in Fermoy could also train a new priest, just like we will be doing here at Saint Timothy's."

"Thank you for your thoughts, Father. Since I'm on the way to Fermoy, I'll leave Father Brown a copy of your syllabus and ask if Saint Michael's would like to participate, alongside Saint Timothy's."

Looking at his watch again, the Bishop said, "I must be going, Father. However short—and I apologize—this visit has been very productive. I knew I could depend on you for a fresh idea. Thank you."

Murphy and the Bishop, both still talking and motioning, walked out to the waiting sedan. Murphy was so engrossed that he did notice the black smoke billowing out a shattered west window.

As the Bishop's sedan pulled away, a red fire engine took its place in front of the church and firemen jumped out and ran inside the chapel.

"Fire, Father! Fire!" Pat, George, and Amos, all shouting, appeared at the kerb. The front door of the church burst open with a loud cracking sound, emitting smoke and heat.

Murphy was restrained by Amos from following the firemen into the church.

"Oh, no! NO!" Murphy implored, still being held back by Amos, now joined by Pat and George.

"Don't go in there until the blaze is contained!" the burly Fire Chief warned as he motioned more firemen through the front door with hoses and axes. "Stay out!"

The growing crowd at the front of the church was joined by three white-faced women. Terrified, Viola, Casey and Kennedy stood there, gaping. Kennedy's body shook so much that her cane was useless and she almost fell. Viola and Casey supported her frail body from both sides.

The smoke-blackened Fire Chief came out the front door, unable to disguise his solemnity. "I've called the police, Father," he said. "There's a burning body in there!"

THIRTY FIVE

"My God!" Murphy exclaimed.

"Forgive me, Lord!" he recovered. "Who can it be?" As he spoke, he remembered Maude was to meet him inside for confession.

He turned to the huffing Inspector O'Bryan and repeated what the Fire Chief had said. "There's a burned body in there according to the Fire Chief!"

"Who is it?" The inspector fitted a gas mask to his face and motioned to several of his constables to do the same.

Another fire truck slid to a stop and more firemen jumped out and began connecting long hoses to the yellow hydrant on the corner.

A medic from the just-arrived ambulance stopped and peered at Murphy's red face. "Sit down, Father. Your face is burned and best be treated immediately." He motioned Murphy to sit on a stretcher while he began applying ointment to the priest's face.

Viola rushed to his side, crying, "Oh, Father! You're burned!"

She clasped both hands to her head and turned to the medic. "Is he alright? Anything except those burns? Shouldn't he be in the hospital?"

"Lady, I can only answer one question at a time. I think he'll be fine if you calm down and keep him out of that burning church."

"I've let Saint Timothy's down," Murphy muttered to himself, walking toward the blackened open front door. "I must administer last rites to whoever is in there."

Viola turned to ask the medic to restrain Murphy, but it was too late. He was already inside the smoking church. Instead, the medic held the arm of the resisting Viola who was trying to follow Murphy.

"Don't be a fool, lady!" With that he motioned to another medic to keep her there. "Tie her down, Sheila, if you have to!"

Inside, Murphy struggled over hoses and around groups of yelling firemen to the confessional near the west wall. Its burned back door had been hacked open by the firemen, exposing a charred form in the penitent's chair.

O'Bryan stopped Murphy from entering. "We'll get the body out later. Whoever it was, is dead already. You can't help him or her now, Father."

"Never too late to save a soul," Murphy whispered so low O'Bryan couldn't hear. He kneeled on the charred floor by the small door, donned the thin purple stole from his hassock and began reciting last rites.

THIRTY SIX

Murphy and O'Bryan sat on the kerb, silently surveying the smoking debris, wreckage, tangled hoses and fire equipment in front of the church. "I'll need a statement, Father."

"Of course."

"To include where you were when the fire began. The Fire Chief estimates that time as 7:30. Who else did you see there?

"Can you identify the body taken out a minute ago? We need help since the body is badly burned. Could be male or female."

"Sorry I can't say who the victim is with certainty, Inspector. I was to meet Maude Connor in the chapel this morning. The Bishop arrived unexpectedly so I didn't see her as planned. The Bishop left just as the first fire truck arrived. I'll ask Viola to check with the Connor home, to see if she's there.

"What caused the fire?" Murphy asked aloud. "The Chief said there was an odor of accelerant. We had a fire inspection just a week or so ago and our rating was satisfactory."

O'Bryan wiped his forehead. "Well, it wasn't satisfactory today. I'm investigating the death as a homicide."

"I expect all the assistance you can give me." He watched the expression on Murphy's drawn face.

"Viola is an excellent observer," Murphy grimaced. "I'll ask her to make a list of everyone here this morning."

The inspector nodded, searching for his pipe. "I think you may be the best observer of all, Father. Who's on your list of suspects?"

"We can exclude the Bishop." Murphy shook his head. "Everybody else—me included—must be on that suspect list."

A later walk-through of the chapel interior took Murphy's breath away. He sat in his usual pew, looking dazed.

The confessional box was the worse. It was just a charred, shattered box. The yellow police tape surrounding it emphasized its blackness. The fire had started in the confessional. A large circle around it of black flooring and pews marked the extent of the major damage. Long fingers of black extended upward to the chapel's ceiling and rafters from the walls. Several old stained glass windows had been blown out by the intense heat.

What was once an old, revered and well-kept chapel was now a ugly, stained curiosity. Amos, the sexton, sat down beside Murphy. "It could have been worse, Father," he tried to sound cheery. "The majority of the chapel is usable once I get it cleaned up a bit."

Viola entered, motioning Amos to scoot over so she could sit beside Murphy. She grabbed his dirty, reddened hand. "We'll restore it, Father. The final result will look even better than the original. Maybe we should consider a city-wide service right here for everyone to see this.

"Saint Timothy's will have a rebirth! Stronger and better than ever!"

With her usual dispatch, Viola penned a list of the people at the church that morning and handed it to a police sergeant. Minutes later, she'd somehow assembled those on her list in a queue outside the parlor where the police interviews would be held. She even enlisted George, Pat and John to gather extra chairs and tables for the interviews.

O'Bryan waved Murphy to his table as a courtesy to begin the interview process. First, Murphy wrote a statement about where and with whom he'd been that morning. The inspector reviewed his statement, asked questions and made marginal notes.

Murphy asked if Viola could be next, so she could begin organizing a cleanup crew to begin in the chapel once the police investigators had finished.

Murphy touched her arm as he left the parlor with the inspector. "Thank you, Viola. You are a treasure!"

Innocently, she looked at him as he was leaving. "Do you mean to you or to Saint Timothy's, Father?"

Murphy, almost blushing, speeded out to join O'Bryan to avoid answering.

O'Bryan motioned Murphy inside the chapel and around the yellow tapes. "Hoping you can help me recreate the murder sequence, Father, since you know this place and these people better than anyone."

"I can only provide guesses, Inspector."

"That's a grand start for my investigators. What do you think happened?"

O'Bryan nodded to a constable taking notes as Murphy began.

"Well, the fire chief estimated the blaze started at 7:30. Shortly before that, Maude Connor may have entered the chapel via the front door, anticipating that I'd be waiting for her here by the confessional."

Looking at his hand, Murphy noticed for the first time the burns covering it. "Since I wasn't here, she probably sat down in a pew nearest the confessional, since that was her reason to be here."

The inspector looked behind him at the constable taking notes. "Getting' all that, Riley?"

The constable hardly looked up to acknowledge the question, continuing to write on a steno pad. "Yes, sir."

"Apparently everyone in the church knew Maude was here and that she was in the chapel. At some point, she must have entered the confessional through this small back door and settled in the chair that used to be inside. I'm presuming that the dead body found there was Maude's.

"Again, I'm guessing, Inspector, at a possible sequence."

O'Bryan nodded impatiently. "Go on, Father."

"The fire chief said there was an accelerant used, probably petrol. When we had that fire and safety inspection here not long ago, a tin of petrol was discovered in a sacristy closet. It could have been used to start the fire."

O'Bryan turned to the constable again, getting a nod about the note taking.

"Show me the closet, please, when we're finished here. What might have happened next?"

"Knowing Connor was inside the confessional, the murderer blocked the closed door with a chair so she couldn't get out. He or she then soaked the walls of the confessional and the immediate floors around it and lighted it."

"A question, Father," O'Bryan scratched his head and sat down in a pew. "Certainly she—if it was Connor inside the confessional—could smell the petrol and sense the fire. She would have called for help as loudly as she could!"

Murphy shook his head, sadly "Confessionals are made to be sound-proof, sir, to assure the privacy of the participant. If that little back door was shut, her cries could not have been heard more than a few feet away."

The inspector stood. "Now, let's take a look now at that closet where the petrol may have come from."

"The petrol tin could have burned in the fire," Murphy opined.

"We'll search the grounds and trash barrels for it. Let's find that closet in case the tin was returned there."

Inside the sacristy, Murphy pointed to and started to open the door of the closet.

"Stop, don't touch that!" O'Bryan blurted. "I'll get the evidence team to open it and search for prints."

The evidence team arrived, searched for prints, eventually nodded to O'Bryan and left with an empty tin. O'Bryan and Murphy peered inside the now bare closet smelling strongly of petrol.

He turned to Murphy. "You said that tin was found on a safety and fire survey?"

Murphy tried to remember the exact date. "Yes, it was."

"Why was it left here, instead of moving it to a safe place?"

"That I can't remember," Murphy admitted. "Is there a chance that there may be finger prints on that closet, the tin or the confessional door?"

"We're checking everywhere for prints, Father. Please drop by the evidence team and let them take yours, too."

Viola met them at the sacristy door. "I just talked to Eunice at the Connor home. Maude left home early this morning. Eunice, the housekeeper, has no idea where she might be. She even left her cell phone in the bedroom.

"It's most strange, Eunice says. Connor never leaves without her car and driver, much less her cell phone even if she's just crossing the street."

O'Bryan and Murphy looked at each other, nodding agreement. "That burned body must be Maude Connor."

The first person to be interviewed after all the statements had been reviewed was Mrs. Kennedy, sitting upright, blackened and stern. Due to her age and fearsome reputation, O'Bryan did the interrogation himself.

He studied his notes and looked up at her.

"Do you understand you are still under oath to tell the truth, the entire truth and nothing but the truth in this official investigation of a murder?"

Kennedy looked angrier. "Of course I understand! Do you take me for a ninny?"

O'Bryan loosened his tie before checking his notes again. "I understand you've mentioned on several occasions your desire to remove Mrs. Connor from Saint Timothy's vestry?"

"I may have *mentioned*," she emphasized his word, "that Maude was our best candidate to be the chairperson of the Castle anniversary celebration. In that capacity, she'd hardly have time for the church vestry."

The inspector made a notation. "Did you make a threat against Mrs. Connor, to the effect 'somebody must stop that woman?"

Kennedy sighed, wondering who had reported that. "I knew your father, Mister Inspector Liam O'Bryan, and I was present at your first communion in Saint Timothy's.

"Now I know you must ask questions about Maude Connor and I intend to answer them as best that I can.

"On your topic of 'someone must stop that woman,' I

was speaking of Maude's intention to have both our priest and administrator transferred to the Aran Isles.

"I ask you, Liam O'Bryan, have you ever heard of anything more heinous? Yes, I'm definitely against Maude's manipulating that silly Bishop or Monsignor into taking such a devilish action against Saint Timothy's!"

She leaned forward into O'Bryan's face. "Wouldn't you feel the same? You're from Saint Timothy's, too, whether or not I see you there every Sunday as I ought."

The inspector cleared his throat again. "I have here your statement of where you were at the approximate time of the murder of Mrs. Connor. You say you were here at the church at approximately 6:45 a.m. Did you see Mrs. Connor at the church when you arrived?"

"No. Before you ask, I was there as soon as I got a call from Viola that both the Bishop and Maude were at the church."

"What happened next?"

"The fire in the chapel, the fire department and you arrived."

"Did you see anyone near the chapel before the fire began?"

"No, but I was in Viola's office, talking and having tea with her. The Bishop left in his sedan about then and that's when the smoke from the fire attracted everyone's attention."

"Do you know anyone who hated Mrs. Connor enough to murder her?"

Kennedy examined her diamond ring before answering. "Lots of folk, both in and out of Saint Timothy's, resented Maude's high and mighty attitude."

"Enough to murder her?" O'Bryan persisted.

"No."

She sat back, tight-lipped, still regarding him as an inquisitor.

Feeling the interrogation roles had been reversed and he was now the perpetrator instead of the questioner, a red-faced O'Bryan stood and, without a word, held the door open for Mrs. Kennedy to leave.

O'Bryan breathed heavily as he shut the door behind her and examined his notes for the next interview. He straightened the uniform tie, cleared his throat and called for the constable at the door.

"John Reilly, next."

He repeated his warning about being under oath. "Murder is a very serious matter, Mr. Reilly. I expect you to answer all questions honestly.

"Now from your statement you and several others were planting small trees on the west side of the chapel. Who was with you and who was first to notice the fire?"

Reilly sat on his hands to hide their dirt from digging. "With me was Pat Davis, George Bailey and, oh, yes, Amos, the sexton came up whist we was diggin'.

"I think Amos was the first to notice the smoke from the chapel. It was so intense and hot that several windows exploded." Reilly nodded at the memory.

"What were your feelings toward the deceased Mrs. Connor?"

Reilly rubbed his chin stubble and looked at the floor. "I didn't have occasion to know the lady."

"Did you ever hear her referred to as 'Her Ladyship?'"

"Oh, that." Reilly smiled with relief. "Lots of people called her that."

O'Bryan shuffled his pages. "I have here a report that

you and two other men in John Long's were heard to say words to the effect 'someone should get rid of that devil.' Is that true, Mr. Reilly?"

Reilly's face colored. "It was just talk among chums over a pint. Just talk. We didn't mean nothin' by it."

"Did you or your chums set that fire in the chapel?"

Perspiration caused John to wipe his forehead. "No, sir!"

"Did you see anyone enter the chapel before the fire started, Mr. Reilly?"

"No, your honor. I did not."

"Have you any idea who might have started the fire that killed Mrs. Connor?"

"I do not, your honor."

It was almost 9:00 p.m. but the Police Station in Mallow was ablaze with light. Wearily, Inspector O'Bryan and three detective-investigators sat around a table comparing notes on suspects in the murder of Maude Connor.

"Beats me, boss," Detective O'Leary exclaimed as he mashed out his last cigarette in an ashtray. "We've got at least three possible killers in the group we've interrogated already. Three!"

"And that's if you eliminate old lady Kennedy," chimed another detective.

"She's as capable of planning and executing this as well as any of the others."

"I disagree," Smith chimed in. "That filled petrol tin weighs almost 18 pounds. That old woman couldn't carry it from the sacristy to the chapel, spread the petrol all about and light it all by herself. She's too weak and spindly."

"Why rule out an accomplice? Maybe Kennedy and

that Viola did it together to get back at Maude Connor. Everybody here seems to despise her."

"Or maybe it was Kennedy and that housekeeper, what's her name?"

"Casey, same name as that lad who tried to burgle the Coffee House, then got smacked on N20 by Connor's big Mercedes."

"Hey! There's motive for you," Flaherty exclaimed, making a note on his pad.

"You said the suspects?" O'Bryan changed the subject. "Seems to me one of those three men planting trees outside the church that morning could have nipped inside while the other two were busy, dumped the petrol, ignited it with a match and run back outside without being noticed."

"There was also a fourth man outside, Inspector," Smith reminded. "That was Amos, the sexton. He was the first to notice the fire."

O'Leary poured himself another cup of coffee. "By the way, that Amos was responsible for storing the petrol in an unsafe location in the sacristy. Yesterday his clothing and gloves smelled of petrol."

"If there were prints on the petrol tin or on that little confessional door, we'd have our murderer."

"Seems to me you're eliminating the priest too quickly," maintained Faherty.

"Flaherty, Father Murphy was with the Bishop from the Bishop's arrival until his departure at 7:30. The Bishop's car left just as the first fire truck arrived."

"Okay, but what about that young female?" Flaherty checked his notes. "Viola Norton? I have a note that she claimed she'd 'do anything to protect Father Murphy in any way possible.'"

"Including murder? Flaherty, you're daft," O'Leary sneered.

"Women will surprise you every time, Mr. Bachelor O'Leary."

"I know," O'Leary countered. "That's why I'm still a bachelor!"

"Where was Norton before the blaze was noticed?"

"According to her statement," Smith picked a sheet out of his stack, "she was on the telephone with Mrs. Kennedy, telling her that both the Bishop and Connor were at the church. That got Kennedy hot-footing over to the church to see what was happening. After Kennedy's arrival, she and Norton were in Norton's office having tea and a chat before the fire broke out."

"Speaking of Norton," O'Leary held up a hand. "Here's a note saying Norton telling Connor that she might come to harm if she did something. What that 'something' is, I don't know."

"Where was the other woman, that Mrs. Casey?"

"She was serving the other two, Norton and Kennedy, their tea."

The inspector yawned. "This seems to be getting us no where. Maybe it was not somebody at the church at all.

"Go home, get a few hours rest and meet me back here at 7:00 with some new ideas."

The others were too tired to protest for a later starting time.

That night three men sat amiably at their favorite table in John Long's. Pat Davis, George Bailey and John

Reilly, unusually silent, finished their first pints and ordered seconds.

"No fun being questioned by the police, eh?" George was the first to speak. "They even made me write out a long, detailed statement about where I was at 7:30."

"Where were you?" Pat snickered and took a sip from his fresh pint.

"With you and John out there planting those little trees! Where'd you think?"

Pat nudged John. "Was he with us the whole time, John, or did he take a break and disappear into the chapel?"

George slapped his hand against the table. "No time for jokes, Pat. This is a murder investigation. Someone blocked that little confessional door, poured out the petrol and set fire to the confessional knowing Maude was inside. Like her or not, the poor soul was burned to death and in our church! Saint Timothy's could have been completely destroyed along with Maude!"

John emptied his pint. "If not one of us sitting here, who did it?"

George held up a hand. "The police told me not to talk to anyone, not even my wife, about my testimony."

"Me, too," Pat admitted.

"This isn't testimony," John argued. "This is speculation. Who did it, I'm asking?"

Pat put money on table for their last drink. "Well, I doubt it could have been one of those three women in the church."

"Three? I thought there were only two, Viola and Mrs. Casey?" George frowned.

"Who was the third?"

"Mrs. Kennedy was in Viola's office, too."

"Rule the women out." Pat objected. "It had to be a man. Could have been Amos. He wasn't outside with us the whole morning."

George again slammed his fist on the table. "Hold on there, Mr. Patrick Davis! I'm not a fan of those detective shows on TV3, but I know there has to be a strong motive for murder. What possible reason would kindly, old Amos have to murder Maude Connor?"

"Got him!" O'Bryan's shout could be heard throughout the police station the next morning. It so startled the detectives standing at the coffee machine that several spilled hot coffee.

"Get in here, men," O'Bryan called from his office. "Quick time!"

Hurriedly, the three detectives took seats around the table, wondering if they were to be reprimanded or rewarded.

O'Bryan waved a single sheet at them. "Listen to this," he cackled. "It's from forensics. They have identified several prints on that petrol tin which began the blaze at Saint Timothy's!"

Three answering voices sounded like one. "Whose?"

"The prints are those of...," O'Bryan savored the delay, watching their faces.

"Amos, the church sexton! Although there are several other smudged, unidentified ones on the tin, his prints are as clear as the Shannon!

"Get out of here! Arrest him, read him his rights and

begin the interrogation. I'll tell the Superintendent we finally have a viable suspect in this case."

To himself, he murmured as the detectives left, "Maybe I should tell Father Murphy, also. But then he'd want to expound to me on his fantasies about who the murderer is."

The evening *Journal* used its largest size type on the front page to announce:

MATRIARCH MURDERED IN CHURCH!

The well-know local matriarch of Mallow's founding family, Mrs. Maude Connor, was found dead yesterday in the burning confessional of Saint Timothy's Church. Although the coroner's report is as yet incomplete, Mrs. Connor apparently burned to death in the chapel during a 7:30 a.m. fire that began in the confessional. A Police spokesman confirmed in this exclusive *Journal* report that an unnamed person believed to be employed by Saint Timothy's has been arrested on suspicion of murder and arson. Investigations by both Police and Fire Department are ongoing.

As soon as he read the article, Father Murphy was on his bicycle, pedaling to the police station. As he left the manse, he noticed Mrs. Casey standing in the garden over a small fire, burning trash. He waved farewell to her but she didn't notice.

On arrival, he waited twenty minutes before Inspector O'Bryan was available. As a constable explained, "We have a murder investigation on our hands, Father. The Inspector will be with you as just as soon as he can."

O'Bryan looked as if he hadn't recently slept but stood as Murphy entered the office and extended his hand. "What may I do for you, Father?"

"I read in the *Journal* that you arrested an employee of Saint Timothy's for Maude Connor's murder. Since our sexton, Amos McPike, is absent, I presume Amos is in custody."

"Correct, Father. We have a forensics report that Amos's fingerprints are all over that tin used to start the fire which killed Mrs. Connor. Also, his clothing and gloves smell like petrol."

"That's to be expected of the poor man, Inspector. He does all the maintenance work around our church. Amos probably uses petrol every day operating machines then cleaning them up."

Murphy drew his hands up, as in prayer. "Surely you can't charge—much less convict—a man on such evidence?"

Red-faced, the inspector leaned back in his chair and reached for a pipe before replying. "In my opinion—my professional opinion—Father, our evidence is solid.

"Perhaps you didn't know he also made a threat against Mrs. Connor, something to the effect 'her day of reckoning is coming.' Eh? Bet you didn't know that."

Murphy shook his head. "You're right. I didn't know that but Maude is not a favorite lady as you now realize. 'Day of reckoning' isn't a real threat to my mind.

"I'm asking you to release Amos to me until you have

221

substantial evidence against him. By then, I'm sure you will have discovered who is the *real* murderer."

With dignity, O'Bryan stood and opened the door of his office. "Good day to you, Father. If you discover some real evidence, please let me or one of my detectives know."

THIRTY SEVEN

That evening, Murphy telephoned Mrs. Kennedy at her home. "You heard the police arrested Amos for Maude's murder?"

"I have," she replied. Without pause, she asked. "What are we going to do about it? I'm more of a suspect than harmless old Amos!"

At his desk, Murphy caught sight of Viola and motioned her into the office.

"Viola and I," Murphy began, as a surprised Viola blinked at him, "have decided we should organize some sort of relief fund for his defense. Perhaps you'd consider making such a motion in our next vestry meeting?"

"Bless you, Father," Kennedy chuckled. "You were always a bright lad. Can we have the vestry together tonight?"

He smiled at her blessing. "Viola's right here. I'll ask."

Turning to Viola, he repeated, "Can we have a vestry meeting to discuss helping Amos as soon as tonight? Or is that too early to notify everyone?"

Viola immediately picked up the other telephone on the desk. "I'm on it," she replied. "Seven o'clock this evening?"

Murphy relayed the hour to Kennedy while Viola began calling the vestry members.

The members began selecting chairs around the parlor table as if it had been the usual, long-planned meeting. Joyce MacDoo, official scribe of the group, began the meeting by announcing "All members are present, Father."

Murphy stood. "Thank you for coming on such short

notice: my fault, not Viola's. May we begin with a prayer for our departed member, Mrs. Maude Connor."

With that, he led them in a short prayer.

"Concerning the late Mrs. Connor," he continued, "I intend to begin a novena in the chapel, as soon as we have it cleaned up, for our late comrade and vestry member. As vestry members, I hope each of you, out of love and compassion for Maude, will be able to attend those short services at 6:00 p.m. Viola will pass the word when we can begin those special services in our damaged chapel."

Viola began speaking as soon as Murphy nodded at her. "Our purpose here is to discuss ways we can assist in the defense of Amos, our sexton, who's been arrested for Maude's murder and the burning of our chapel.

"Any ideas?"

Pat Davis was first. "Makes sense to take a special offering for Amos at the novena services for Maude, doesn't it?"

Mrs. Kennedy objected. "That doesn't sound appropriate to me. Our attention and prayers at novena should be on Maude, not Amos, as much as we like him.

"How about another parade to the court house, as we did protesting that trial of Maude's driver, Jim Summers?"

George Bailey raised a hand to be recognized. "All that's to the good," he said, "but we need to do something before Amos is officially charged for the crime by the Director of Public Prosecutions."

All eyes turned to George. At least two people blurted the same question. "Like what?"

"The police contend that Amos was with us planting those willow trees when the blaze was discovered…"

"Before 7:30," John added.

"Yes, John, before 7:30," George grinned at his chum's enthusiasm. "But did the police ask where Amos was prior to 7:30? If he started the fire, that's when he would have done it."

Murphy picked up a pen and opened his notebook. "Where might Amos have been before 7:30, George?"

"I think Amos was riding that truck delivering those willow saplings to the church. If I'm correct, Amos is innocent of starting the fire. He wasn't even here until 7:30, hanging with the three of us outside." George looked at Pat and John and got their nodding agreement.

"That's brilliant, George!" Pat exclaimed. "I bet the police didn't ask Amos where he was earlier. I know he was dazed and confused by all their questions."

"And frightened," Mrs. Kennedy added.

"George, you and I should go to the police immediately and tell them what you just said. It might save Amos from being charged. Could be, he'll even be released!"

The others applauded as Murphy and Bailey left the parlor.

Over his shoulder, Bailey shouted. "We'll meet all of you at John Long's within the hour to celebrate!"

"If it's a celebration, I'm buying the first drink!" Kennedy yelled.

Not to be outdone, quiet Joyce MacDoo hooted. "And I'm buying the second!"

It was almost ten o'clock when Father Murphy and George Bailey stepped into John Long's bar with raised hands signifying victory. The vestry members all applauded, amid raised pints and tall glasses.

"Amos may be released from jail in the morning!"

George brayed, while motioning to the bartender for two more pints.

"Inspector O'Bryan said Amos would be interviewed again and questioned about delivering those willow trees. If it is as we said, Amos can go home, free and clear!"

Viola made room on her bench for Murphy. "Sit down, Father. This is an extraordinary meeting of Saint Timothy's vestry. Maybe all our meetings should be here, at least until the debris is cleared from the chapel."

"If Amos is released tomorrow, we can put him on organizing our chapel cleanup," Murphy tasted his drink.

Viola touched her pint to his. "We have a group of volunteers organized already, Father."

Murphy grinned as he took another gulp. The others cried, "Your health, Father!" Murphy saluted them with his pint.

Afterward, Viola and Father Murphy walked together back to the manse. Midway there, Viola stopped. "Father, I have something I must say but I'm troubled about bothering you at a time like this."

"Viola, you and I are both workers for Saint Timothy's. You can tell me anything. Do you have confession in mind or something else?"

"Something else, Father."

"Perhaps it would be easier to tell me in the morning, after you've had a good rest?"

"Oh, no, Father. I'd certainly lose my courage if I delayed."

Once at the manse, Murphy gestured toward the bench in front. "Would you like to have a seat here and get it off your mind? That way perhaps you can rest more comfortably tonight."

"Thank you, Father, for your understanding. As usual," she balked, "I don't know where to start systematically."

He patted her hand. "Then just blurt it out, Viola."

"Father, I said a very bad thing to Maude. I told her she was sure to come to harm if she tried to get you discredited over the Summers trial."

Viola breathed heavily. "There, I said it! Please forgive me!"

"Of course, I forgive you. I appreciate your confidence in me."

"But that's not all!" she persisted.

"Go ahead."

Viola took another deep breath. "Mrs. Casey told me she hoped Maude would burn in hell! And Maude did burn!"

Murphy sat back, frowning. After a second, he said. "Thank you for telling me."

"Will you tell the police, Father? I guess I should have done that already."

"Leave it to me, Viola. I'll think of some way to get Mrs. Casey to discuss her feelings without mentioning you. Maybe I'll inform the police after that."

Viola rose from the bench and inclined her head to Murphy. "I feel much better already, Father. Thank you. Thank you."

She entered the manse, leaving Murphy deep in thought on the bench.

THIRTY EIGHT

After breakfast that morning, Mrs. Casey stuck her head into Murphy's open door where he was preparing notes for the first of the novenas. "Good morning again, Mrs. Casey. Thank you for that fine breakfast."

Casey looked perturbed.

"What's wrong?"

"It's the police, Father. They're here wanting Miss Norton."

Murphy bounded out of his chair, "I'll be right there."

In the anteroom, Detective O'Flaherty stood, hat in hand.

He began immediately. "Inspector O'Bryan ordered me to bring Miss Norton in for questioning about the Connor murder, Father."

On hearing her name. Viola came to the office door. "What?"

"Miss Viola Norton?"

"Yes."

"I'm to escort you to the police station where you will be further questioned about the recent fire and murder in the chapel."

Murphy interrupted. "Is Miss Norton being arrested?"

"No, Father. She's just asked to accompany me to the station for more questioning."

Seeing her alarm, Murphy reacted. "Get your purse, Viola. We won't be long,"

O'Flaherty held up a hand. "Sorry, Father. The Inspector was very specific that I am not to bring you with her."

Murphy shook his head. "Then I'll follow you on my bicycle. Don't worry, Viola. This is sure to be a misunderstanding. I'll tell Mrs. Casey to delay lunch preparations."

At the station, they were met at the door by Inspector O'Bryan, glaring at both O'Flaherty and Murphy. "This is police business, Father, you should not have come."

Murphy glared back. "Miss Norton is a brave young lady, Inspector, but your methods are likely to upset her. I'm here to offer pastoral as well as friendly support during her interview. Or is this an interrogation?"

"No need for such a tone, Father. We have a murder on our hands and, thanks to your tinkering, one suspect has been released."

"Establishing the truth is never 'tinkering,' Inspector. To assure Miss Norton's being treated fairly, I intend to sit with her during her 'interview.'"

"Sir, you may not join or interfere with her interview."

"Then I insist on being interviewed separately, just like her. My corroborating interview should convince you of Miss Norton's innocence in this tragic affair."

O'Bryan blocked the door, barring Murphy's entrance into the interview room with Viola and a detective.

"Oh, all right!" he said, plainly exasperated. "You'll be interviewed as soon as we're through with her."

"Thank you."

Detective O'Flaherty conducted Murphy's interview an hour later. "You understand that this interview is being recorded and may be used in a court of law against you?"

"Of course. Before you begin, Detective, where is Miss Norton now and what is her condition?"

"She's fine, Father! We didn't torture her! She's sitting in the canteen with a female constable having tea and biscuits. She's fine," he repeated.

"Very well. If I may, I will tell you what happened that terrible morning and where Miss Norton was during the entire period. May I begin?"

O'Flaherty turned on a recorder "If you object to being recorded, say so."

"No objection. First, allow me to describe our normal early morning routine at the manse. Habitually, we all arise at 6:00, dress, have private prayers and meet for breakfast at 6:30. After breakfast, Miss Norton and I review our daily schedules and any changes we need to make.

"At 6:45 that morning I received a telephone call from the deceased. The gist of our conversation was that she desired the sacrament of confession. She also was very specific. It was to be in the small confessional in the chapel as soon as possible that morning. Mrs. Connor and I agreed to meet at the confessional in thirty minutes, so I went to the chapel to prepare and pray before her arrival.

"Miss Norton left the dining table where I'd just been when Mrs. Casey, our housekeeper, told her that Bishop Hagen had just arrived at the front of the church at 7:00. His Excellency made a surprise visit to us at Saint Timothy's. Viola met the Bishop out front and explained I was in the chapel. She escorted the Bishop to where I knelt in the first pew. He joined me for his own prayers, after which we went to my office. There we discussed a proposal I'd made for the training of newly ordained priests assigned to the diocese.

"Miss Norton went back to her own office and telephoned Mrs. Kennedy with the extraordinary news of the Bishop's surprise visit and that Mrs. Connor was here as well. As our senior vestry member, Mrs. Kennedy felt obliged to come to the church to greet the Bishop. She arrived within minutes and she and Miss Norton had tea in the dining room I had just left, since the Bishop and I were conferring in my office.

"I estimate that Mrs. Connor arrived at the church around 7:15 and entered the confessional, closing its door behind her, while waiting for me. Since I was unexpectedly talking to the Bishop, she had to wait several minutes beyond our agreed meeting time of 7:15.

"At 7:30 the Bishop departed from the front of the church in his sedan when we saw flames and smoke erupting from within the chapel. The Bishop left without seeing the fire. As soon as the Bishop left, a fire truck skidded to a stop in front of the church.

"So, you see Miss Norton was within a few feet of me from 6:30 until she left the Bishop and me in the chapel. Thereafter she was with Mrs. Kennedy in the dining room until the fire was noticed at 7:30 and eventually extinguished by the Fire Brigade.

"Viola Norton was with me or Mrs. Kennedy during the time in question of the fire and murder, which I place at 7:15 to 7:30. I think this interview, if you compare it with hers, proves Viola is innocent and should be immediately released."

Another half hour passed while Murphy waited outside the inspector's office. When he emerged, O'Bryan appeared still agitated at the familiar sight of the priest.

"Your point is well taken, Father," O'Bryan sputtered,

choosing his words. "Miss Norton appears to be innocent of the fire and murder. She may return to the church but may not leave Mallow without police permission in case we have further questions for her."

"Thank you, Inspector. Since I arrived on my bicycle, could she be returned to Saint Timothy's in the vehicle which brought her here?"

A stiff nod was O'Bryan's reply.

As Murphy helped Viola into the police sedan, Murphy offered encouragement to the embattled O'Bryan. "I hope to have new evidence for you shortly, Inspector, with which you can close this case."

With that, Murphy climbed onto his bicycle and followed the police sedan down the street toward Saint Timothy's.

Inspector O'Bryan stood there, rubbing his forehead, both bewildered and encouraged by Murphy's parting words.

THIRTY NINE

A happy Viola trounced into her office at Saint Timothy's to find Mrs. Kennedy sitting there.

"Close the door, please," was Kennedy's greeting.

Nervously, the older lady began. "Mrs. Casey told me you'd been taken away by the police, dear. Are you alright? What did they ask you about? Anything about me?"

Rather than immediately answer, Viola slumped in her chair and laid her head back. "What a relief! Here I am, safe and sound, thanks to Father. Were it not for him, I'd still be there, probably locked up for weeks."

Viola sat up. "They reviewed my previous statement, the one everyone gave. Where was I, who was there, that sort of thing. I don't remember their mentioning you, Mrs. Kennedy."

Kennedy sighed. "I imagined they'd ask you about what I said about Maude at one of our vestry meetings."

"What did you say?

"I said "Somebody should stop that woman."

Viola wrinkled her nose. "I'd also said something about 'she was sure to come to harm if she tried to discredit Father Murphy.' They even knew I said that! Imagine!"

For the first time, Kennedy smiled. "Hopefully, we both passed their test."

Viola reached for the telephone. "We should celebrate! Let's have a nice steaming pot of tea!"

Before the tea pot was empty, the two ladies were in the chapel, checking the clean-up of the burned area where the confessional had been. Bailey, Reilly, Davis and Amos had hauled out the debris of the confessional. They stood there, looking at the burned wooden flooring where the confessional had been.

"What can we do about that, Amos?" Pat Davis asked.

George Bailey added, "And before the first of the novena services this evening?"

The church sexton looked about the room and walked to the front. "That'll do," he murmured.

He pointed. "That big rug beneath the Bishop's chair ought to cover the burned floor. Let's haul it down here and see."

Their chore completed, three of the men headed out the door, then over to John Long's bar. They claimed their favorite table, soon were all smiles while holding cold pints of stout.

John Reilly nudged George, sitting beside him. "I thought Amos was coming with us?"

"He wanted to, but Father had another chore for him as we left the chapel."

"I thought the chapel looked clean enough for the novena this evening, didn't you?"

Pat nodded, adding, "Amos can tell us later what his special job was. Another three pints, Sean!"

Father Murphy lit his pipe and blew smoke at the flies on the office ceiling, before calling Mrs. Casey on the house telephone. "Bring us a bit of tea, won't you?"

In a few minutes, she was at the open door. Murphy took the tea tray from her and set it on the desk. "I've been meaning to ask you how Joe is recuperating at the hospital?"

"Fine, Father," she sat across from him, cup in hand. "Thank you for askin'."

"Perhaps I could visit him tomorrow?"

"He'd like that, Father, as would myself."

Murphy put aside his pipe and tea cup. "I've been meaning to speak to you for some time, Mrs. Casey. It's about your future."

She gasped. "What do you mean, Father? Is my work falling off? Are you in mind to fire me?"

"No, not that. I have been praying for you to seek confession, to cleanse yourself of malicious thoughts and actions committed to others, specifically Maude Connor.

"I hope you plan to attend the novena for her this evening?"

Casey's hand shook so that she replaced her cup on the desk. "No, Father, I don't plan to come. I hated her for what she failed to do for my Joe when her car struck him down on that highway and," Casey grabbed a tissue from the desk, "left him there like he was garbage."

"That's why I've been praying for you to come to confession," Murphy whispered. "Your words tell me you must seek absolution and freedom from your mortal sin.

"I want you to kneel with me right here and confess that sin, Mrs. Casey. Now's the time to rid yourself of that burden."

Murphy looked her in the eyes. "Now, Mrs. Casey. Now," he insisted.

"Before it's too late."

Even Murphy was startled by her reaction. Wailing, she dropped to her knees beside him on the floor.

"Bless me, Father, for I have sinned mightily. It's been two months since my last confession. I am heartily sorry for what I did to that woman and the chapel."

"Tell me your actions for which you seek absolution."

Casey hesitated. "Can you assure me that the seal of the confession will be unbroken by you, Father?"

"I assure you that what you are about to confess will be an absolute secret known only to you, me and God."

"Well, then," she trembled. "I confess I killed that woman. I knew she was in the confessional, waiting for you. You were delayed by the arrival of the Bishop."

She took a deep breath and clasped her hands. "I stuck a chair against that little door so she couldn't get out, then I doused the petrol on the door and all around the confessional.

"I lit it with a wooden match and ran back to kitchen, hearing her screaming as she burned. God help me!"

She stopped and looked at him through her cupped fingers. "Did you know I did it, Father?"

"Yes, my daughter. I suspected it when I saw you burn your petrol-soaked scullery gloves in the garden."

Casey wiped away tears with another tissue. "Will the police know?"

"If not immediately, yes, they will eventually know. Not from me but from the film in that security camera in the chapel rafters. Amos removed the camera and gave it to them this morning."

Oh, Father! You've condemned me!"

"No, Mrs. Casey. The judge may condemn you to an earthly prison. I am concerned about where you will spend eternity.

"I absolve you from your sins in the name of the Father, and of the Son, and of the Holy Spirit. Give thanks to the Lord for He is good."

"My God! What will happen to Joe if I go to prison?"

Murphy stood and helped her to her feet. "Amos needs

an assistant. Joe will be fine, but you must continue praying for him, yourself and Saint Timothy's."

Inspector O'Bryan stood beside the door and silently acknowledged Murphy as he took Mrs. Casey to the police car outside.

The first novena was attended by over twenty people and seemed uplifting, even to the vestry members who knew Maude Connor too well. Afterwards, Viola and Murphy sat in the manse dining room with sandwiches and tea.

"I apologize for your scanty supper, Father."

"Please don't, Viola. This is fine. I don't expect you to cook for us now that our housekeeper is gone."

"I know, Father. That kind Mrs. Kennedy is sending over her own housekeeper in the morning. But Father…"

"Yes?"

"I can cook, too, and intend to show you just how well. Remember my lamb stew?"

They smiled at each other.

TICKLER

The growing crowd at the front of the church was joined by three white-faced women. Terrified, Viola, Casey and Kennedy stood there, gaping. Kennedy's body shook so much that her cane was useless and she almost fell, Viola and Casey supported her frail body from both sides.

The smoke-blackened Fire Chief came out the front door, unable to disguise his solemnity. "I called the police, Father," he said to Murphy. "There's a burning body in there!"